THE BOOK OF COMMON PRAYER

INCLUSIVE AND LOVING MODERN PRAYER FOR THE CHURCH AND CLERGY

Part of the first SAFE religion Series

The first SAFE religion series presents a version of the Christian faith that is guaranteed to be loving, inclusive, unprejudiced, non-discriminatory, non-sexist, non-racist, non-violent, not homophobic, enlightened, peaceful, modern, uplifting, challenging and of use to all Christians and all denominations.

THE BOOK OF COMMON PRAYER

INCLUSIVE AND LOVING

MODERN PRAYER

FOR THE

CHURCH AND CLERGY

Archbishop Jonathan Blake

Text copyright © Archbishop Jonathan Blake 2021

Bishop's Haven
105 Danson Crescent
Welling
DA16 2AS
U.K.

ISBN-13: 9798780818533

archbishopjonathanblake@gmail.com

DEDICATION

Dedicated to my dearest ones

Annette
Nathan, Dominic, and Gabriel

Table of Contents

INTRODUCTION 1
MORNING PRAYER 4
EVENING PRAYER 12
THE CREEDS 19
NIGHT PRAYER 21
HOLY COMMUNION/MASS/JESUS'S SUPPER 32
AN EASTER COMMUNION 45
A CHRISTMAS COMMUNION 53
A MEAL OF LOVE FOR THE WORLD 61
THE BAPTISM OF A CHILD 71
A NAMING AND BLESSING SERVICE ... 88
THE CATECHISM 96
BAPTISM AND CONFIRMATION OF AN OLDER CHILD OR ADULT 103
EQUAL MARRIAGE LITURGIES 113
FUNERALS 153
DIACONAL ORDINATION 159
FOR PRIESTLY ORDINATIONS PRECEDED BY A BRIEF DIACONAL ORDINATION 175

FOR PRIESTLY ORDINATIONS 177

THE CONSECRATION OF A BISHOP 191

THE 39 ARTICLES OF MODERN CHRISTIANITY 206

THE AUTHOR'S BIOGRAPHY 217

INTRODUCTION

This book of inclusive, loving, and modern prayer is not meant to be prescriptive but liberating. Too often, similar books have become instruments to stifle creativity, by requiring conformity and dutiful adherence and repetition.

Not so this book. It will hopefully be a useful resource to help point the way towards a more inclusive form of worship, prayer, and ritual. More, I hope it will release people from a sense that what has been, must always be, and what they have received, cannot be altered.

Instead, this is an example and an invitation to all, to be bold, creative, experimental, and expansive. No one should feel bound by precedent, nor by the words and ways of those before them.

Naturally, our heritage is of great importance, educating us and resourcing us, but it must not deter us from fulfilling our destiny. We must play our part in contributing to the evolution of the understanding and practices of Christianity.

Much of the language and many of the liturgies of the past have become disassociated from society and the common experience. Worse, they have become offensive and representative of past oppressive attitudes and prejudices.

It is essential we are bold in revising and reforming the Christian faith, if it is to retain its relevance, play a significant role in maintaining the common good and inform our quest to establish a just, equitable and harmonious world community.

Feel free to use these liturgies, alter, adapt, amend, and improve them. Make them your own. Write entirely new ones. Allow the Holy Spirit to unlock the infinite potential within us all, to speak our truths and discoveries for today's world.

There is nothing that needs to be done, or said in a particular way, other than to always ensure, that everything is done and said in a loving manner and for love's best.

I will be re-editing this book continually and I ask for your help in so doing. If you have suggestions for a better way of expressing something or a different observation that you think should be included or just a technical, grammatical, or other observation, please email me them, for my consideration.

I have not specified psalms or readings for the services or included a lectionary. I have published a safe version of the New Testament and the Psalms, and they can be used in conjunction with this prayer book.

How many psalms you say or readings you include is for you to decide. Better to be adaptable, than to burden yourself with a required schedule. Each day, the time available and your own mood brings differences, that flexibility can happily accommodate.

Prayer and worship, at best is inspirational, comforting, healing and empowering. It should not be something that grinds you into dependency and a resentful observance.

Love is essentially sensitive, always looking to achieve the best for everyone. Hence, no liturgy, ritual, dogma, doctrine, service, or system should ever be allowed to damage people. If something is going to do that, change it.

MORNING PRAYER

Introduction

O Love, open our lips

And our mouths will express our thanks

Song of Praise

Because of Love

Let us call aloud

To this rock of our salvation

Let us offer our thanksgiving

And extol Love with music and song

For Love is supreme

And Love reigns over all

The depths of the earth

And the mountain peaks

The sea and the dry land

Come, let us offer our praise

Let us be in awe at all of creation

We are Love's gift

And Love cares for us all

Glory be to the Creator, the Redeemer
And the Sanctifier,
As it was in the beginning,
Is now and shall be for evermore

Invocation

The darkness has given/is giving way to the light
Let us leave behind the fears and torments
Of the night
And be filled with Love, hope, compassion
Kindness, and forgiveness

YOUR CHOSEN PSALM/S ARE SAID

Canticle

Blessed are they who are not
Influenced by the wicked
Nor choose to do wrong
Nor surround themselves with the cynical

Instead, they find delight in the ways of Love

And meditate on doing good, day and night

They will be like trees

Planted beside streams of water

Burgeoning with fruit when the harvest comes

With verdant and lush foliage

They will find their efforts rewarded

For Love will ever watch over and guide

Those who seek righteousness

Glory be to the Creator, the Redeemer

And the Sanctifier,

As it was in the beginning,

Is now and shall be for evermore

YOUR CHOSEN SCRIPTURE AND OTHER READINGS

Canticle

Give thanks to Love

For Love has blessed us

Rescued and redeemed us

Love has given us new birth

And protected us from all dangers

And from all that has been against us

Love has strengthened us

And brought us new life

And summoned us to be good and loving

All the days of our lives

And you, beloved

Will do marvellous things

You will be motivated by Love

And go before Love to prepare Love's way

You will provide people

With a deeper understanding about Love

And inspire them to confess their wrongdoing

And seek forgiveness

Love shows such mercy upon us

As the sun rising to shed its light

And bring its warmth

Shining on those who are living in darkness

Guiding our feet into the paths of peace.

Glory be to the Creator, the Redeemer

And the Sanctifier,

As it was in the beginning,

Is now and shall be for evermore

Jesus's Prayer

May Love be revered

May unity come

Good will be done

That earth may become our heaven

May we work hard for our daily needs

And may our wrongs be forgiven

As we forgive those

Who have done wrong to us

And may we not fall into temptation

But be delivered from evil

For we believe in Justice, Truth, and Peace

RESPONSES

May Love show mercy upon us

And assist us in our times of need

May the world's leaders be guided by righteousness

And may we live in truth and with integrity

May all those with responsibility act honourably

And may each of us play our part in bringing others joy

May Love save us

And bring justice, peace, and equity to all

May we be blessed by peace

And do our utmost to establish and preserve peace upon the earth

May Love cleanse us, heal and empower us

And may we be blessed by Love's goodness within us

THE THREE COLLECTS

FIRST - YOUR OWN SPECIAL PRAYER FOR THE DAY

FOLLOWED BY:

May Love guide, resource, and inspire

Us to work for peace

To give ourselves in the service of others

To be tireless in reaching out to help the weak

And assist the needy, the alienated

And the ostracised

And to be protected from all those

Who would attack us

Trusting always in Love's defence

Amen

We give thanks to Love

For bringing us safely

To the beginning of a new day

May we guard against

Temptation and danger,

And act wisely and selflessly

With the intent and hope

Of enhancing and benefiting

The lives of others

Amen

The Conclusion

So may we arise

To meet all the possibilities of the day

With renewed vigour and resolve

And may Love be with us

EVENING PRAYER

Introduction

O Love, open our lips

And our mouths will express our thanks

Song of Praise

Sing happily because you are loved
Lift your hearts in joy and gratitude
Make music with the voices of many instruments
Sing new songs, compose new tunes
And shout with delight
For Love is right and true
Faithful in all things
Love leads to righteousness and justice
Unfailing Love is all around
This miracle in which we live
The open skies, the star lit nights
Oceans gathered in the pockets of the earth

Molten lava roiling deep below

We should all be riveted in awe

Everyone transfixed by existence

Glory be to the Creator, the Redeemer

And the Sanctifier,

As it was in the beginning,

Is now and shall be for evermore

Invocation

The evening is upon us

And yet opportunities for the light remain

Embolden us with zest

To use well the hours ahead

That we may be lights

In the darkness of this world.

YOUR CHOSEN PSALM/S ARE SAID

CANTICLE

Love's mercy is over all of creation

From generation to generation

Love performs mighty deeds

Love challenges the proud

Love removes the power from unjust rulers

Love lifts the humble

And while the rich may know dissatisfaction

Love will fill the hungry with good things

Glory be to the Creator, the Redeemer

And the Sanctifier,

As it was in the beginning,

Is now and shall be for evermore.

YOUR CHOSEN SCRIPTURE AND OTHER READINGS ARE READ

Canticle

Love, giver of life

I can finally close my eyes in peace

For I have seen Love's hope of salvation

Found in the birth of children

A light that continues to shine

Throughout every generation

The chance of attaining paradise

Glory be to the Creator, the Redeemer

And the Sanctifier,

As it was in the beginning,

Is now and shall be for evermore.

Jesus's Prayer

May Love be revered

Unity come

Good will be done

That earth may become our heaven

May we work hard for our daily needs

And may our wrongs be forgiven

As we forgive those

Who have done wrong to us

And may we not fall into temptation

But be delivered from evil

For we believe in Justice, Peace and Truth

RESPONSES

May Love show mercy upon us

And assist us in our times of need

May the world's leaders be guided by righteousness

And may we live in truth and with integrity

May all those with responsibility act honourably

And may each of us play our part in bringing others joy

May Love save us

And bring justice, peace and equity to all

May we be blessed by peace

And do our utmost to establish and preserve peace upon the earth

May Love cleanse us, heal and empower us

And may we be blessed by Love's goodness within us

THE COLLECTS

Lighten our darkness

Love we pray

And in your mercy

Protect us

From all the perils and dangers

Of this night

That goodness may prevail

And hope overcome

And when the labour of this day is ended
And our rest has come
We may lay ourselves down in peace.
Amen

May Love avail for all those in need
Through the hours ahead
That those attending to their care
May be strengthened
And those who are without help
May, in the mystery of this world's suffering
Yet, in time, know relief and restoration

Amen

The Conclusion

We arise to meet the coming night
With a burning, undiminished light
Thanks be to Love.

THE CREEDS

THE APOSTLE'S CREED

I believe in God
Creator of heaven and earth
I believe in Jesus Christ
Who was born of Mary
He suffered under Pontius Pilate
was crucified, died, and was buried
He descended to the dead
On the third day Love rose again
I believe in the Holy Spirit
the holy Christian Church
the communion of saints
the forgiveness of sins
Love's resurrection
and life everlasting. Amen.

THE NICENE CREED

I believe in one God
Maker of heaven and earth,
And of all things visible and invisible
And in Jesus Christ
God of God, Light of Light
Very God of very God
Who for us, and for our salvation
Was incarnate by the Holy Spirit
Born of Mary

He was crucified under Pontius Pilate
He suffered and was buried
And the third day Love rose again
According to the Scriptures
And I believe in the Holy Spirit
The giver of life
And I believe one Christian and apostolic Church
I acknowledge one Baptism
For the remission of sins
And I look for Love's Resurrection
And the life of the world to come
Amen.

NIGHT PRAYER

Introduction

Love grant to us a quiet night and a perfect end

Our help is in the name of Love

Who is the creator of all

Confession

We are sorry

And ashamed

Of the wrongs

We have thought

And said and done

And the harm we have caused

We pledge

To put things right

And live anew

And forgive others

And hope to be forgiven

Amen

Responses

May Love be quick to save us

May Love make haste to help us

Glory be to the Creator, the Redeemer

And the Sanctifier,

As it was in the beginning,

Is now and shall be for evermore.

SONG

Before the ending of the day,

Creator of the world, we pray

That you, with steadfast love, would keep

Your watch around us while we sleep.

From evil dreams defend our sight,

From fears and terrors of the night;

Tread underfoot our deadly sins

That we no wrongful thought may know.

Creator, that we ask be done
Through Jesus Christ, your loving Son;
And Holy Spirit, by whose breath
Our souls are raised to life from death.

Psalm/s – say one or more

Please hear me when I cry out

O source of life and Love, relieve my distress
Have mercy upon me and hear my plea.
For how long will others try to shame me
For how long will they be allured
By lies and deceit
They will discover that Love
Provides a protection for me
Love hears when I call
So tremble and refrain from wrong
Lying on your bed, enter the silence

Examine your heart

Commit to doing good

And allow yourself to trust

Many are obsessed with wealth

But true wealth is found in the light

May my heart be filled with joy

At all the blessings received in abundance

I will lie down and sleep peacefully

Because Love allows me to dwell in safety

Glory be to the Creator, the Redeemer

And the Sanctifier,

As it was in the beginning,

Is now and shall be for evermore

Whoever dwells

In the shelter of Love

Will rest in the shadow of Love's embrace

I will say, "Love is my refuge

And my safe haven

The one above all else

That I trust"

Surely Love will save us

From the traps laid for us

From the deadly diseases

Love will cover us with feathers

And under Love's wings we will find refuge

Love's faithfulness will be our protection

And our defence

We will not fear the terror by night

Or the weapons used by day

Nor the dangers that stalk in the darkness

Nor the plague that destroys at midday

A thousand may fall at our side

Many thousands further beyond

But the danger will not come near us

We will watch carefully

And see the consequences of corruption

If we say, "Love is our refuge"

And we make Love our home

No harm will overtake us

No disaster will threaten our household

For the powers of goodness

Will guard us in all our ways

Their hands will bear us up

Over the presenting dangers

Lest we fall and are dashed against the rock

Or are endangered by wild beasts

Or fall victim to those

Who would strike us with poison

We will walk safely over all these dangers

Love says, "I will rescue the good

Who are faithful and loving

I will protect them

For they honour my name

They will call on me

And I will answer them

I will be with them in trouble

I will deliver them

And bring them honour

With long lives

I will satisfy them

And show them my salvation"

Glory be to the Creator, the Redeemer

And the Sanctifier,

As it was in the beginning,

Is now and shall be for evermore

Let us praise Love

All the good people of the world

Who work tirelessly for Love

Night and day

Lift up your hands in thanks

And praise Love

May Love bless you

The Love that created all that exists

Glory be to the Creator, the Redeemer

And the Sanctifier,

As it was in the beginning,

Is now and shall be for evermore

YOUR CHOSEN SCRIPTURE AND OTHER READINGS

Or

Be sober, be vigilant, because your adversaries, temptation and evil, prowl around you like roaring lions, seeking whom they may devour. Resist them, strong in faith and Love.

Responses

Into Love's hands, I commend my spirit

Into Love's hands, I commend my spirit

For Love has redeemed me, giver of truth and light

So, I commend my spirit

Glory be to the Creator, the Redeemer

And the Sanctifier,

As it was in the beginning,

Is now and shall be for evermore

I commend my spirit

Keep me as the apple of Love's eye

Hide me under the shadow of Love's wings

Love, giver of life

I can finally close my eyes in peace

For I have seen Love's hope of salvation

Found in the birth of children

A light that continues to shine

Throughout every generation

The chance of attaining paradise

Glory be to the Creator, the Redeemer

And the Sanctifier,

As it was in the beginning,

Is now and shall be for evermore

Invocation

May Love save us while waking

And guard us while sleeping

That awake we may watch with Love

And asleep we may rest in peace

Prayers

May Love visit this place, our homes, our hearts
And drive away all the snares of evil
That we may abide in tranquillity
And rest in safety
And know Love's sweet and healing blessing upon
Us through the night hours.

The Conclusion

In peace we will lie down and sleep

For Love alone makes us dwell in safety

May Love abide with us

For the night is at hand and the day is far spent

As the night watch looks for the morning

So do we look eagerly for Love

May Love come with the dawning of the day

And be made known in the breaking of bread and the sharing of food and drink

Love bless us and watch over us

May Love's face shine upon us

And be gracious to us

May Love look kindly on us and give us peace

HOLY COMMUNION/MASS/JESUS'S SUPPER

Love be with you.

And also with you

Confession

(Here we pause to reflect silently on the ways in which we are unaligned as individuals and as communities)

Loving God

We acknowledge our wrongdoing

Misdeeds, and culpability

We are truly sorry for our part

In damaging others

Ourselves and creation

We intend to do our best

To put things right

Make amends

And live anew

Amen

Absolution

God who is Creator
Redeemer and Sanctifier
Bless, preserve, and sanctify us
May the divine look kindly upon us
And be gracious to us
May Love absolve us from all our sins
And grant us the grace and comfort
Of the Holy Spirit.

THE COLLECT – YOUR CHOSEN SPECIAL PRAYER

The Gloria

Glory to God in the highest
And peace to all people on earth.
Loving God
Heavenly Monarch
Almighty God and Creator
We worship you
We give you thanks
We praise you for your glory

Loving Jesus Christ

Cherished Child of God

Loving God

Lamb of God, you help take away

The sin of the world:

Have mercy on us

You, who are revered and honoured:

Receive our prayer.

For you are the Holy One

You are the Saviour

You are High and Exalted

Jesus Christ

With the Holy Spirit

In the glory of God, the Supreme. Amen.

YOUR CHOSEN PSALMS, SCRIPTURE AND OTHER READINGS

Your prayers

THE THANKSGIVING

God be with you

And also with you

Lift up your hearts

We lift them to the highest

Let us give thanks to our all-loving God.

It is right to express our thanks and praise

It is indeed, right
And our delight and our joy
To gather in unity
And celebrate the miracle of life
The wonder of creation
Love's transforming power
And the privilege to serve.
Awakened by Love
And blessed by grace
We laud and magnify your glorious name
Evermore praising you and saying:

Holy, Holy, Holy God,
God of all creation
Heaven and earth are full of your glory
Hosanna in the highest

Blessed is the one who comes in the name of God

Hosanna in the highest

This is a blessed day
A day for life-giving renewal
When the sun of hope
Burnishes at full strength
Rays flaring like the mane of a lion.

On this day we will raise
The bread of profound Love
And glimpse the eternal drama
Of life, death, and new life
As we are drawn
Into the power and struggle
Of God's Spirit in the world.

Our unique planet brims with possibility
This is a day for rejoicing
For fruitfulness and creativity
For imagination and innovative thinking
For celebrating the fire in our spirits
And finding our compasses set at true

As we venture on in our journeys.

But light creates the shadows
The flourishing and the diminishment
And the secrets that lurk in the darkness
Are destined to be revealed

And in this place of revelation
And exposure
Where all can be known
And the truth confronted
We embrace with love
All that is broken in our world at this time........
All who are suffering .....
All who are sick ......
All who are....

And we place ourselves
At the heart of the divine rhythm
Where life encounters death
And overcomes through Love
To rise anew

For Jesus was born

In the milk and moon of earth
pushed from the dark nascent waters
into a divided world

He was seen with eyes
And touched with hands like our own
There was road-dust on his feet
Sea-salt in his hair
The grime of toil behind his fingernails

And beside the waters
And on verdant slopes
He touched hearts, opened minds
Loved, helped, and healed the people
And challenged corruption

And gathered around a table
On a night of foreboding and fear
He took bread in his hands
And blessed it
He broke it
And said,
"Take and eat
For my body too, will be broken

Out of my Love for you all
And when you so eat, in the future
Remember me."

He then took a pitcher of wine
And poured it into a cup.
He blessed it
And said,
 "Drink this
For my blood too, will be poured out
Because of my Love for you all
And when you so drink, in the future
Remember me."

And in travail and torment
And with blood soaked sweat
He took his lonely path
To the place of the skull
While birds sang, and orchards blossomed
And rivers wove their gentle way
Curving through the folds
Of the heaving land

And atop the roiling depths beneath

He hung alone upon a tree

Rooted in the bare soil

Amidst the dereliction and despair

Encompassed by darkness

Betrayed, bereft and bewildered

He was cast violently into the abyss of loss

Deep down into the darkness of shame

Into the silence, and suffering

To the place of annihilation and negation

Where the Spirit of Love

Was undeterred

Restoring and resurgent

Light, hope and life imparting

Rolling away all the brokenness

Flooding night's grave chamber with day

Liberating the tomb's captives

Speaking words of hope

Reconnecting, redeeming, and reconciling

Words issuing from the eternal womb

Giving birth again to possibility

Summoning us all to our senses

Inviting us to be so filled with Love's Spirit

That Love would arise within us

Flow through us,

Motivate, guide, and empower us

Making us kind and compassionate

Bearers of healing to the languishing

And committed, in Jesus's name,

To play our part

In building a just, good

And peaceful world.

Challenged, inspired

Humbled and hopeful

We give our thanks and praise.

JESUS'S PRAYER

May Love be revered

Unity come

Good will be done

That earth may become our heaven

May we work hard for our daily needs

And may our wrongs be forgiven

As we forgive those

Who have done wrong to us

And may we not fall into temptation

But be delivered from evil

For we believe in Justice, Peace and Truth

AGNUS DEI

O Lamb of God, who helps take away the sins of the world

Inspire us to continue your good work

O Lamb of God, who helps take away the sins of the world

Enable us to continue your good work

O Lamb of God who helps take away the sins of the world

Grant us your peace and Love's power

SIGN OF PEACE

The peace that Jesus gives be with you

And also with you

Let us offer each other the sign of peace.

The Mingling

May this food bring life, in all its fullness, to those who receive it.

Jesus helps take away the sins of the world. Blessed are those who share the food of Love's table

I do not feel worthy to receive such Love, but only say the word, and I shall be healed.

PRAYER AFTER COMMUNION

We thank God for the gift of this divine meal and for the gift of each other.

Blessing

May God bless us with discomfort at easy answers, half-truths, and superficial relationships, so that we may journey deeply into the meaning of life.

May God bless us with indignation at injustice, oppression, and exploitation, so that we may work for justice, freedom, and peace

May God bless us with tears, for those who suffer pain, rejection, hunger, or war, so that we may reach out our hand of comfort, providing love and compassion.

And may God bless us with enough foolishness to believe that we can make a difference in the world, that we can do what others claim cannot be done, and give our lives to helping provide justice, and peace for all.

All: Amen

Dismissal

Our service is ended. We may go in peace and Love.

Thanks be to God.

AN EASTER COMMUNION

God of grace
Your Love, as known in Jesus
Has the power to break
The chains of death and hell
And fill us with faith and hope
A new day has dawned
And the way to a new life
Has opened before us
Through which we walk
In celebration and in joy.
Amen

God be with you

And also with you

Lift up your hearts

We lift them to the highest

Let us give thanks to our all-loving God.

It is right to express our thanks and praise

New life has erupted from the grave

The wonder of creation, refusing to be bound
Love's transforming power
Taking the raw materials of our choices to destroy
And fashioning them into opportunity and hope

And we experience
unexpected forgiveness
Inclusion and belonging
We are awakened by Love
And blessed by grace
So we laud and magnify your glorious name
Evermore praising you and saying:

Holy, Holy, Holy God,
God of all creation
Heaven and earth are full of your glory
Hosanna in the highest

Blessed is the one who comes in the name of God
Hosanna in the highest

This is a unique celebration
Of the rising son

Inflamed at full strength
Rays flaring like the mane of a lion
And inspired, warmed, and healed
We too are rising
And holding high
The bread of profound Love

Enthralled by the eternal drama
Of life, death, and new life
Engaged in the struggle
Of God's Spirit in the world
We have been confronted
With the power and presence
Of evil around us and within us
Found ourselves complicit
Conduits of decay and
Exposed at Golgotha

Our pretensions of innocence
Falling silent
Amidst the nailing and the taunting
That cauldron of hatred and harm
That we had mixed and stirred
And even now

We, with trepid step
Remember:

All who are suffering .....
All who are sick ......
All who are....
So many, held in hell's grasp
Desperate for help

Yet our unique planet brims with possibility
With fruitfulness and creativity
With imagination and innovative thinking
As Love is resurgent
We celebrate the fire in our spirits
Find our compasses set at true
We venture on in our journeys.

And we place ourselves
At the heart of the divine rhythm
Where life encounters death
And overcomes through Love
For Jesus was born
In the milk and moon of earth
Pushed from the dark nascent waters

Into a divided world

He was seen with eyes
And touched with hands like our own
There was road-dust on his feet
Sea-salt in his hair
The grime of toil behind his fingernails
And beside the waters
And on verdant slopes
He touched hearts, opened minds
Loved, helped, and healed the people
And challenged corruption

And gathered around a table
On a night of foreboding and fear
He took bread in his hands
And blessed it
He broke it
And said,
"Take and eat
For my body too, will be broken
Out of my Love for you all
And when you so eat, in the future
Remember me."

He then took a pitcher of wine
And poured it into a cup.
He blessed it
And said,
 "Drink this
For my blood too, will be poured out
Because of my Love for you all
And when you so drink, in the future
Remember me."

And in travail and torment
And with blood-soaked sweat
He took his lonely path
To the place of the skull
While birds sang, and orchards blossomed
And rivers wove their gentle way
Curving through the folds
Of the heaving land

And atop the roiling depths beneath
He hung alone upon a tree
Rooted in the bare soil
Amidst the dereliction and despair

Encompassed by darkness
Betrayed, bereft, and bewildered
He was cast violently into the abyss of loss
Deep down into the darkness of shame
Into the silence, and suffering
To the place of annihilation and negation

Where the Spirit of Love
Was undeterred
Restoring and renewing
Light, hope and life imparting
Rolling away all the brokenness
Flooding night's grave chamber with day
Liberating the tomb's captives
Speaking words of hope
Reconnecting, redeeming, and reconciling
Words issuing from the eternal womb
Giving birth again to possibility
Summoning us all to our senses

Inviting us to be so filled with Love's Spirit
That Love would arise within us
Flow through us,
Motivate, guide, and empower us

Making us kind and compassionate

Bearers of healing to the languishing

And committed, in Jesus's name,

To play our part

In building a just, good

And peaceful world.

Challenged, inspired

Humbled and hopeful

We give our thanks and praise.

A CHRISTMAS COMMUNION

At this time, at the brink of a new creation
Of the pulse of a new life
And of a birth that brims with hope and promise
Showing how the darkness and the difficulties
Can be overcome
When we celebrate the assurance
That we can prevail
When our hope is replenished
And our resolve strengthened
We give thanks for all those who have risen
From the ashes of destruction
And with wings of love
Have soared high
Inspiring, leading, and empowering others
So that we can all play our part
In transforming, enlivening
And improving our world,
For the benefit of all.
In Love's name,

All. **Amen.**

Love be with you
And also with you.

Lift up your hearts
We lift them high.

Let us be ever thankful
It is right to be forever grateful

It is indeed, life enhancing and true to celebrate all that is good, and filled with promise and opportunity, in our glorious world. The miracle of birth humbles us. From such mysterious, fragile, and tiny beginnings we have evolved and emerged and taken our place in the pilgrimage of all people questing for meaning and purpose.

Therefore, with the company of all who have gone before and those who walk with us today, we unite our voices in common joy as we say:

ALL: We are in awe of our lives, tugged to this earth and its dispensation from unknown quarters, and our lives brim with gifts received, breath imparted, and hope instilled. In wonder, affirmation, and acclamation we say, sing and declare our grateful thanks.

EUCHARISTIC PRAYER

And so we celebrate the miracle
And mystery of birth
At Christmas
When in the cycle of the temperate seasons
Nature lies down to rest
And the bare trees and brooding skies look down
When the flaming sun distantly visits
Before plunging us again towards the gloom

Within this gestation
We raise the symbols of birth
Death and re-birth
And become one with all who are caught
In the birth pangs of the world

The cold earth is awaiting its time
Harvests to come, soft fruits, honey and blossom
But for now alone the icy grasp
The pause before the promise
A time for a different form of gathering
Of sharing and of dreaming
As we hold our breaths
And wait for that which is beyond our control
And even our imagining

And amid winter's long shadows
The unforgiving winds, the encompassing mists
And the bitter air
We empathise with all those who know affliction
And suffering on our perilous earth

...so many in a tormenting array of crises and catastrophes.......especially those far from home, refugees, and asylum seekers, those entrapped by and prey to people smugglers, those in terror aboard flimsy vessels on perilous waters, or encased in metal containers, refrigerated and forgotten, and those whose loved ones have fallen victim to the quest to find a better life away from tyranny, poverty and bloodshed....

We embrace them in our hearts

Yearn for them in our souls
And commit to them in our endeavours

And now it is
Despite the all-consuming shadows
For us to share in the irrepressible dance
Of the universe and the cycle of hope
To marvel at the birth and the death
And the rebirth of which we are all a part

For the person Jesus was born on straw
Homeless, a refugee
Crossing the waters of uncertainty
Between worlds, in flight and in search

There were those who held him
Smelt him, lay close beside him
Those upon whom his tears fell
And over whom his laugh soared
Those with whom he bathed
Ate and drank

And those who gathered round a table
Caught in the complex matrix of current events
When fear, betrayal, and possibility
Burgeoned around them
And as storm waves rocked their upper room idyll

He took a loaf in his hands and blessed it
He broke it and said

"Just as my body is to be broken
Just as many bodies have been broken

And will yet be broken
For righteousness sake
And all of them given for you
And for all people
And in sharing in this collective memory
Please remember."

He took then a pitcher of wine
And poured it into a cup
He blessed it and said

"As my blood will be poured upon this earth
As so much blood has flowed from so many lives
And will yet flow, for righteousness sake
All of it shed for you and for all people
And in sharing in this collective memory
Please remember."

And there in the hush of the night
When darkness cradled good and evil
The cries of a woman in labour
Echoed across the constellations
And swaddling cloths
Brought warmth
Even while a furtive plot brought chill
And the body that a mother had cherished
Prepared for tearing
And the blood that a womb had protected
Awaited its shedding

This child, come of age, the son star
Illumining the galaxies
And the innermost reaches of our minds

Scattering the prevailing darkness
And confounding all trickery and subterfuge
Bearing a gift that surpasses
Value, desire and need
That enriches and transforms us

Upon rude manger straw
In that in-between uncomfortable place
Where only beasts and burdens roamed
It was, that Love, took its first breath
And the dank stench of death
Had no more dominion
And a child uncurled its fingers
To embrace our hearts
With a touch that imparted life and hope
And a bearded man stretched wide
Those hands to absorb the nail shaft
And make it glint with light

No more this old dispensation
Where horizons are cramped
And our songs are muted
Where hurt hugs the walkways
And tears sodden our paths
In birth all becomes new
Another invitation to press the soft earth
Dancing to a different rhythm
Awakening time and destiny to the eternal
Reaching out beyond ourselves
To fashion a new earth that gently encompasses
All that is, within the whole
That in peace we can celebrate.

For shepherded to safety
And enthralled by heavenly music
Beside our animal friends and all of nature
In awe at the simplicity
And poverty of our preparations
And overwhelmed
At the inexpressible value of the gift
Caught up and implicated in the unfolding drama
We receive that which has been transformed
That we might ourselves be changed
Rising, replenished, and renewed
To incarnate Love in our lives
And bring to birth
A new dawn, a new hope, and a new world.

Blessing and honour and glory and grace be this gift of life releasing love. Amen.

PRAYER AFTER COMMUNION

We give thanks for life
For this time together and for each other
Nothing now need ever defeat us
Discourage or deter us.
Strengthened by our solidarity
With the suffering and the
Friendship of all those involved
In the quest to achieve peace and justice
We will proceed with unlimited reserves of hope
Love and forgiveness to make the dream of
Universal happiness and freedom come true
And may all that is good come to our aid.

The Blessing:

May Love lift us from the place of fear
Isolation and dread and release within us
A tsunami of hope and positivity
That we may re-engage with our lives and all life
Reborn, renewed, replenished, and restored
Pilgrims of love, generously sharing
Unconditionally, the love that has brought us joy
And may the God of all Love
Bless each of us
All of our loved ones
And all that lives within this extraordinary
And magnificent created order.
Amen.

A MEAL OF LOVE FOR THE WORLD

Introduction

We invite everyone, from every faith, philosophy, and background, to share this meal of unity, friendship, and hope.

Let us join our hearts and lives in common purpose to build a better world.

Let us turn our backs on the arguments and conflicts of the past and join our hands and wills to protect, preserve and perpetuate life in all its fullness, and help establish and preserve peace and justice upon the earth.

Confession

> We have wounded Love's grace
>
> We have fallen short of our best
>
> We are sorry
>
> And ashamed
>
> Of what we have thought

And said and done

That was wrong

And has caused harm

May we resolve

To put things right

And live anew

And may we forgive others

And be forgiven

SONG OF ACCLAMATION

Glory to Love in the purest

And peace to all forms of life

We praise

We bless

We adore

We glorify

We give thanks for all that is good

Love, justice, truth, and peace

Kindness and mercy

Good people, from all ages

Faiths and cultures

Our inspiration and our light

Who help take away the wrongs of the world

Embolden us

Who help take away the evil of the world

Guide us

Who are held in the greatest respect

Inspire us

For you are to be revered

Honoured and remembered

Shining lights, urging goodness on

Through every generation.

YOUR CHOSEN READINGS

THE THANKSGIVING

Love is all around us
Love's spirit is within us

Let us unite in Love's endeavour
And join our hearts as one

Let us express our thanks and our joy
It is a time to celebrate and remember

We are alive.

We are children of the earth.

We lift our hearts in

Thanks, and praise.

We have discovered the grace of Love.

We have seen acts of

kindness and goodness.

We have witnessed the inspiring

And heroic actions of others.

We respect those who have played

Their part in seeking to

establish a world of justice and peace.

We bow our heads in honour

Of the brave and the true.

Praise, respect, glory, and honour

Be to those who have

given their best and offered their all.

We give thanks for every good thing

That we have received

For hope in times of despair

For light in seasons of darkness

For comfort in the valley of suffering

We give thanks

For those who reach out to help

And to rescue

The lost and the lonely

The poor and the homeless

The broken and the bereaved

As we gather in the spirit

Of friendship and love

And pledge ourselves

To work tirelessly for a better world

We remember all those

Who have suffered and suffer

For the cause of righteousness.

We remember all those

Who have opened wide their hearts

And sacrificed their lives

Who have been tortured

Imprisoned and murdered for noble ends

whose flesh has been torn

And whose blood has been spilt

That others might taste

A sweeter future and know a brighter end

We remember all those

Who have gathered

With their family and friends

Before their ordeal unfolded

Who broke bread, shared food

And who drank

In affection and solidarity

In taking this bread and tearing it

In taking this drink and pouring it

We join with them

Partaking of their plight

Identifying with their suffering

Pledging our commitment

To work to realise their dreams

Of a better world

That their suffering may not be in vain

In sharing, we are nourished

By their example

And become one with them in the struggle

Of all good people to change this world for the better

So, we commemorate the suffering of the innocent

May this meal of memories

And this food and drink of Love

Open our eyes and set our hearts on fire

to unite with all good people

That right may prevail

May Love, truth, justice, goodness, and peace

Fill our hearts, our homes, and our world

Prayer

May Love be revered

May Unity come

Good will be done

That earth may evolve into heaven

May we work hard today for our daily bread

And may our sins be forgiven

As we forgive those

Who have sinned against us

And may we not fall into temptation

But be delivered from evil

For we believe in justice, truth, and peace

EVERYONE IS INVITED TO RECEIVE

THE FOOD AND DRINK OF LOVE

CONCLUSION

Nothing need ever defeat us

Discourage or deter us.

Strengthened by this meal

The solidarity of the suffering

And the friendship of all those involved

In the quest to achieve

peace and justice

We will proceed

With unlimited reserves

Of Love, hope, and forgiveness

To make the dream of universal happiness

And freedom come true

And may all that is good

Come to our aid

THE BAPTISM OF A CHILD

As people are gathering, it is good to mingle, discover as many of the children's names as you can. Perhaps blow bubbles as you circulate. It entrances the children and creates special moments to be photographed.

It provides a magical lead into the service, blowing a bubble, and explaining how fragile our dreams are, and how wonderful it is, when our ultimate dream of having a child becomes a reality.

It is important from the start to include and pay equal attention to the other children of the family, who have already been baptised, to ensure they do not feel excluded or resentful if they are of an age to appreciate or need this.

To start the service, try and obtain a recording of a special song that uses the child's name. A useful link is: https://makemethestar.com/ *and the CD 'Jesus Loves me'.*
It is good to begin with the song (N Jesus loves you...). It surprises and charms the child and children and all those gathered. The CD has ten such songs on it and I give this to the family at the end.

Introductory Petition

Asked of all those gathered

Are you willing to cherish this child, to surround her/him with Love and nourish her/him with goodness? Are you willing to set for her/him the finest example? Are you willing to do your best to inspire her/him by your choices, your words, your actions, and your kindness to her/him in your lives?

WE ARE WILLING.

Here a biblical or other story can be told in a child centered, captivating and imaginative way. As animals are involved in the Noah story for instance, hand puppets can be used, as they are an endearing resource for engaging children's attention and involvement.

A careful and enlightened reference can be made to the story of Noah's Ark and the flood, ensuring that it is presented in a gender balanced and inclusive version, of a family acting wisely, in the face of impending danger, to rescue themselves and their animals and as many others as they could, rather than as a story of God's judgement etc.

It can be linked to the experience of the 10-year-old, Tilly Smith, in 2004, saving many lives through her wisdom, initiative and courage, when Thailand suffered a tsunami. This event also links because the animals then indicated anxiety and sought rescue. The art is to link a modern censored version of the biblical narrative with a modern life experience.

These stories/or others can be linked to the rainbow.

If possible, and when circumstances allow, the use of a rainbow can be introduced. From a black case (indicating the dark storm clouds), long strips of material of the various rainbow colours, tied at one end, can be produced. This can be simple or at best form a large and impressive rainbow effect.

A godparent or other can be asked to hold the gathered end, while the children can be invited to stretch the strips of coloured cloth out among those gathered.

When the rainbow is displayed invite them to sing along with you:

Red and yellow and pink and green
Purple and orange and blue
We have made a rainbow, made a rainbow
(Say the name of the child being baptized)
We have made a rainbow for you.
And everybody here
Yours friends and family
Will guide you safely through
And when you see a rainbow
Colourful, magical, rainbow

Remember we love you

Then you can ask the children what, is said, to be found at the end of a rainbow. When the answers come mentioning gold etc, reveal a gold vessel, and ask what they think could be in it – prompting them, that it is wonderful, special, valuable and amazing – answers given may be money, jewels, sweets, airpods!

Then say, "It is far better than any jewel, any amount of money, any electronic device etc....

Then produce from the vessel a photograph of the child being baptized, with the words:

"(-) is the most treasured part of her/his Mum and Dad's lives." *(If there are other children in the family, their photographs can also be lifted from the gold vessel.)*

And addressing all the other children:

"And all of you are the treasure at the end of your Mum's and Dad's rainbows.

Then invite the following words to be said by the godparents and parents.

Every rainbow is God's promise of Love that the storm clouds will give way to the sunlight, and the colours of life, will spread once more across our lives.

Then the prayer:

Gracious God, you want us to know Love, trust Love and show Love. May we surround (-) with Love and protect her/him from evil, that s/he may be filled with the Holy Spirit, and learn to walk with us, where Jesus walks, in the ways of goodness, justice and truth. Amen

Invite the godparents, should they wish to say something personal or contribute something, like a reading or poem of their choice

The Questions of Commitment

If the 'Godparents' come from a different faith tradition or an agnostic, or atheist approach, or they just want to ensure the questions match their understanding and views, then what is asked of them, during the baptism, can be specially and appropriately written.

Otherwise, these can be used

Do you turn to Christ?

I turn to Christ

Do you repent of your sins?

I repent of my sins

Do you renounce evil?

I renounce evil.

The signing of the child with the cross

Engage the children again, using the oil of the Catechumens, to convey the mystery and resource of faith. On top of the oily wadding in the vessel, place shining stars and invite the children to catch a falling star as you tip them out.

Explain, that when all the help on earth appears to have been insufficient, that they can kneel beside their beds and look out at the stars and know that help will be provided, they need only persevere, trust and hope.

Invite them to sing along with you, "Twinkle Twinkle little star..."

Then,

I sign you with the cross, the sign of Christ, Love's kiss from heaven.
Jesus will walk before you, keeping you safe.

And follow behind you, guarding your path.
Be found ever at your right hand and at your left, your friend, and your inspiration.
And will ever hold your heart, safe within Love's own.

(If there are other children of the family, of an age not to be embarrassed, who have already been baptized, softly sign them too, to include them, with an explanation that you are providing them with a 'top up'.)

The Godparents and parents say:

(-) may we guide you to resist the forces of darkness, in the strength and confidence known in Jesus, and help you learn how to follow faithfully, the paths of compassion and kindness, that lead to life and fulfillment.

Then invite the parents and godparents to sign the child on the forehead with their finger alone, or to place their hand on their head or just to give them a kiss or momentarily place their hand on them whatever is appropriate and possible, but only what is appreciated by the child.

Invite the grandparents and others, including children, to come and bless the baby and invite the parents to take the baby to where any less mobile relatives are sitting.

Play appropriate music during this time.

It is a lovely visual montage if you can obtain a banner covered with coloured hearts or some such, and have the godparents or children either hold this behind the parents and child being baptized or in front of them, as a sign of all the love with which they are being surrounded and supported.

Then take a large jug of water (if there is time and opportunity, you can have hidden the jug beforehand and invite the children to search for it) and a portable font or receptacle and use the water as a further means of enchanting the children, pouring it from a height, so that it splashes them with droplets. Draw closer to the baby being baptized and pour the water more carefully, allowing them to enjoy the sound of the water, the sight of the bubbles created and the gentle splashes. Pour some gently over her/his fingers.

Then fill the font.

Then offer this or your own prayer of blessing.

Loving God, thank you for today, for family and friends gathered in celebration. In oftentimes a complicated world, the chance to laugh, love and delight in all that is good.

Thank you for (-). For their unique and precious life, given to us for our cherishing.

Thank you for water. For the times we play in it, have fun with it, allow cheeky waves to tickle our toes on sandy shores. Thank you for our thirst quenched, our bodies cleansed, our crops watered, and our bodies created, from these crystal streams.

Yet, as well as bringing life, this same water teems with danger, taking many lives. It is a potent symbol of life and death, hope and peril.

And today we thank you for Jesus, that good, kind, and loving man, who transformed people's lives, challenging corruption, healing the broken, respecting the children and pointing us all to the hope of building a new society of justice and peace.

Too good for this world, evil came and stole his life, and the tears began to fall, enough to flood the earth, a tsunami of suffering to drown us all. But in the mystery of resurrection, Love, undeterred, irrepressible, rose from that place of death and hopelessness, to inspire us all to play our part in overcoming evil with goodness, and despair with hope.

So come Holy Spirit and bless these crystal waters with life and grace abundant, that as they sprinkle (-), s/he may be filled with new life, in all its fulness and shine as a light in this world to bring joy to many.

The parents and godparents are asked:

Do you believe and trust in God, the creator of heaven and earth?

I do so believe and trust.

Do you believe and trust in Jesus Christ, whose Love challenges and transforms us?

I do so believe and trust.

Do you believe and trust in the Holy Spirit who inspires and empowers us to live good and loving lives?

I do so believe and trust.

Then ask this question to the parents alone:

Will you love your child and care for her/him; will you always accept her/him and seek to understand her/him; will you always be there for her/him, through the twists and turns of her/his life, helping and supporting her/him through the dark places and laughing with her/him in the light; will you give her/his mind wings with which to fly and will you teach her/his heart to soar; will you lead her/him upon gentle paths and give her/him a love for truth and justice; will you cultivate in her/him a deep compassion for others and a respect for her/himself; will you show to her/him the beauty of this world and cover her/him in the sunlight of all that is good?

We will

Then invite the parents and godparents around the font, as well as any other children of the family, if they wish. If the child to be baptized is hesitant, take the font to the child. If they are becoming distressed, take a break, or make a game of it, or proceed in such a discreet way that the child doesn't realise it is involving them.
Invite other children to gather round too, making sure they do not obscure the view of others.
Play with the water to start, allowing the baby/child/children to place their fingers and hands in it.
Us a smaller dish to collect some of the water so you can pour it, making bubbles and bathing the child's hands with it.
If there are several children in the family, (even if some are not being baptized), ask them to place their hands one under their other, each under their sibling/s pair of hands, and then pour some of the water over the top pair of hands and watch it trickle down like a waterfall to the font.

You can accompany this, with words akin to:

These are the hands you helped create, that your love brought to the world.

You could invite the child to put some of the water on their parents.

Now check whether the parents want you to hold the baby or not. If it is a child they can stand, and if too small, on a stool or some such.

Then, at an appropriate point baptize the baby/child, saying the appropriate words, trying your utmost to do so in a way that causes no distress but is part of the happiness being experienced. At best, it is a seamless part of the water play. They may even reciprocate! If they do appear anxious, try using the smaller vessel you have, to pour water into the font as a distraction, while you administer the tiniest amount of water to the baby/child with your other arm, out of their sight.

If the child is older, you can ask whether they want a sprinkle or a soaking! If a soaking, cast an eye to the parents for advice and then administer what is an appropriate amount to the occasion. If a lot, (making sure it is a hot day or the child can change their top) and have a towel to hand.

Having baptized the baby/child, say the words:

I deliver her/him to your earthly care. Tend her/him well for s/he is your child of love and there is nothing more precious to you in the whole world, than (-), *and add the names of any other children of their family.*

If the service has not been too long, and if it seems appropriate, you can anoint the baby with the oil of Chrism. Again, connecting with the children, filling the pot with silver hearts, and inviting the children to catch one as they tumble from the pot.

Not having to touch the baby, but signing near the relevant area, one can say words such as:

Let your eyes be opened to see all manner of beauty. Let your ears be opened to hear the words of the wise. Let your lips speak words of kindness. Let your hands do good things upon the earth and let your feet bear you upon the paths that lead only to life.

Then taking a baptismal candle and lighting it, and holding it at a safe distance from the baby

One can sing:

This little light of mine
I'm going to let it shine
(x3)
Let it shine(x3)

Then say:

I give you this light because Love's light has filled you.

The parents and godparents say:

(-) Let the light of Love shine from within you, guiding your choices, giving hope to others, and leading you to live a good, compassionate, and productive life.

Then encourage the parents and godparents to regard the anniversary of the baptism as a second birthday, when the baptized was 'born again'. So, to relight the candle each year and for the godparents to send cards and a gift for their godchild. If appropriate, you can even invite everyone to sing Happy Birthday to them. Then invite the baptized, or if not old enough, the other children or the parents to blow out the candle, and make patterns with the rising smoke, again to intrigue the baby/child/ren.

Then invite the parents and godparents to say:

(-) God has received you by baptism into the church. We welcome you as part of the worldwide family of good people. We belong

together and are the living presence of Jesus. We are daughters and sons of the one God. We are inheritors together of Love's promises, and Love's invitation to help change this world for the better

Jesus's Prayer

May Love be revered

May unity come

Good will be done

That earth may become our heaven

May we work hard for our daily needs

And may our wrongs be forgiven

As we forgive those

Who have done wrong to us

And may we not fall into temptation

But be delivered from evil

For we believe in Justice, Truth, and Peace

Bless, we pray (name/s of the parent/s and child/ren), that their home may be filled with light, Love, security, and happiness. May they build together a welcoming home, open to the needs of others, and able to engage with, but not be damaged by, our complicated world. May (name/s of child/ren) know a childhood of delights and grow in grace and confidence to equip them for the unfolding of her/his/their unique life/ves.

So may Love bless you all and keep you, May Love shine upon you and be gracious to you, May Love look kindly on you and give you peace and the blessing of the all loving God, creator, redeemer and sanctifier, be with you, all those who you love, and this entire created order, now and forevermore.
Amen

Finish by singing:

God's got (name of child/ren) in Love's hands (3)
God's got the whole world in Love's hands.

Then after filling the smaller vessel with the baptismal water, sprinkle all the children happily as you sing

God's got all of you children in Love's hands (3)

God's got the whole world in Love's hands.
God's got everybody here in Love's hands (3)
God's got the whole world in Love's hands.

A NAMING AND BLESSING SERVICE

May peace and love and happiness be with you all, today and always.

I call to the North
Powers and creatures of Earth
I call to the East
Powers and creatures of Air
I call to the South
Powers and creatures of Fire
I call to the West
Powers and creatures of Water
Greet this child
And give her/him your blessings

As (Name) grows up s/he needs the help and encouragement of the family, so that s/he learns how to live in a good and creative manner.

CHILDREN LEARN WHAT THEY LIVE

IF (-) lives with tolerance
    S/he will learn to be patient

IF s/he lives with encouragement
    S/he will learn to be confident

IF s/he lives with praise
    S/he will learn to appreciate

IF s/he lives with fairness
   S/he will learn about justice

IF s/he lives with security
   S/he will learn to have faith

IF s/he lives with approval
   S/he will learn to like herself

IF s/he lives with acceptance and friendship
   S/he will learn to find love in the world.

(Parents' names), (Name) whom you have brought for naming and blessing, depends chiefly on you for the help and the encouragement s/he needs. Are you willing to give it to her/him by your example?

WE ARE WILLING.

Where did you come from (-) Dear?
Out of the everywhere into here.

Where did you get your eyes so true?
Out of the sky as I came through.

What makes the light in them sparkle and spin?
Some of the starry twinkles left in.

Where did you get that little tear?
I found it waiting when I got here.

What makes your forehead so smooth and high?
A soft hand stroked it as I went by.

What makes your cheek like a warm white rose?
I saw something better than anyone knows.

Whence that three-cornered smile of bliss?
Three angels gave me at once a kiss.

Where did you get this pearly ear?
Love spoke, and it came out to hear.

Where did you get those arms and hands?
Joy made itself into hooks and bands.

Feet, whence did you come, you darling things?
From the same box as the cherubim's wings.

How did they all just come to be you?
Love thought about me and so I grew.

But how did you come to us, you dear?
Love thought about you and so I am here.

Let us now say together,

**(-), MAY YOUR LIFE BE FILLED WITH LOVE.
MAY YOUR DAYS BE FILLED WITH HAPPINESS.
MAY NO DARKNESS ECLIPSE YOUR LIGHT
AND MAY YOU GROW SECURE AND CONFIDENT,
SURROUNDED BY THE LOVE OF YOUR FAMILY
AND YOUR FRIENDS.**

(Parents' names) have the beautiful and challenging responsibility of guiding (-) in the paths of goodness and light. Is it your desire and hope to bring your daughter/son up to resist those things which are harmful, and to live a wholesome and productive life?

IT IS

(Name of chosen person, or persons), you have been chosen by the family to bear a special responsibility of care and thoughtfulness towards (-). Through your friendship and example s/he will be nourished and blessed. Is it your desire to fulfill this role now and for all your days?

IT IS

(Special people) do you promise to encourage (-) to fulfill her/his dreams and ambitions and to offer your guidance and support when it is needed?

WE PROMISE

Do you promise to be there when s/he needs you, to offer your help, love, friendship and understanding to her/him whenever you can?

WE PROMISE

Do you promise to keep her/him safe from harm and keep her/him in your thoughts?

WE PROMISE

Do you promise to support their parents in her/his upbringing whenever your help and assistance are called upon?

WE PROMISE

Then everyone gathers around the baby/child and their parents into a circle and rainbow colours are woven around them

I anoint you with the oil of blessing, gift from the stars.

I comfort you with the milk of love, flowing from the bosom of creation.

I cleanse you with the waters of life, crystal streams promising light and hope.

As you receive abundant blessing and love, allow your life to issue forth beautiful energy and grace upon the earth and never be ashamed to stand up for what you believe to be right and good.

AND TO LIVE YOUR LIFE IN SUCH A WAY THAT IT WILL BRING HAPPINESS AND BLESSING TO OTHERS AND TO YOURSELF.

May the all loving one protect you and walk beside you through each and every day of your life. Amen

And a woman who held a baby against her bosom said, speak to us of children and the voice said

Your children are not your children.
They are the sons and daughters of Life's longing for itself. They come through you but not from you, and though they are with you, yet they belong not to you.

You may give them your love but not your thoughts, for they have their own thoughts.
You may house their bodies but not their souls,
For their souls dwell in the house of to-morrow, which you cannot visit, not even in your dreams.

You may strive to be like them but seek not to make them like you. For life goes not backward nor tarries with yesterday.

You are the bows from which your children as living arrows are sent forth. The archer sees the mark upon the path of the infinite and bends you with all might that the arrows may go swift and far.

Let your bending in the Archer's hand be for gladness; For even as the arrow that flies is loved, so also the bow that is stable.

You have brought this beautiful girl/boy child to be named. Would you bring her/him into the circle of love?

What is the name that you have chosen for your daughter/son?

Will you love her and care for her/him; will you always accept her/him and seek to understand her/him; will you always be there for her/him through the twists and turns of her/his life, helping and supporting her/him through the dark places and laughing with her/him in the light; will you give her/his mind wings with which to fly and will you teach her/his heart to soar; will you lead her/him upon gentle paths and give her/him a love for truth and justice; will you cultivate in her/him a deep compassion for others and a respect for her/himself; will you show to her/him the beauty of this world and cover her/him in the sunlight of all that is good?

<u>WE WILL</u>

Then I name this child, (-). I inscribe her/his name upon the ground that this earth will provide a safe haven for her/his dwelling and that her/his feet will find safe paths for her/his journeying. I deliver her/him unto your earthly care. Tend her/him well for s/he is your child of love and there is nothing in all of creation which is more precious to you.

May the Divine bless you, keep you and protect you. The sun will bring you light by day and the moon by night but may Love's light be forever bright within your heart and soul.

(-) I give you this candle that you may shine as a light in the world.

AND THE LIGHT OF OUR LOVE WILL SHINE UPON YOU TO WARM YOU AND TO GUIDE YOU. WE ARE YOUR FRIENDS AND YOUR FAMILY AND WE WILL ALWAYS BE HERE FOR YOU.

We hold her/him high to the heavens:

We thank you from our hearts for the life of (-). Look after and protect her/him all her/his days to come and may s/he grow into a fine and good person bringing help and kindness to many. May her/his parents be blessed with ever deepening love and her/his home be filled with joy and peace and her/his future bright and ever blessed.

THE CATECHISM

To be understood by all being confirmed

Question. What is your Name?

Answer. N.

Question. Who gave you this Name?

Answer. My parents, and it was affirmed by my Godparents in my Baptism; wherein I was blessed by God and the Christian community.

Question. What did your Godparents promise for you?

Answer. They promised three things in my name. First, that I should renounce all evil and the vanity of wickedness, and all that is wrong. Second, that I should believe in God the creator, the redeemer, and the sanctifier. And third, that I should keep God's holy will and commandments, and walk in the same all the days of my life.

Question. Do you believe what they promised?

Answer. Yes, and by God's help I will faithfully fulfil the same. I thank God, that my eyes have been opened to the grace that can save me.

Catechist. Rehearse then your belief.

Answer. I believe in God, maker of heaven and earth. And in Jesus, who was born of Mary. He suffered under Pontius Pilate, was crucified, died, and was buried. On the third day, Love rose again from the dead. I believe in the Holy Spirit, the church, the communion of saints, the forgiveness of sins, Love's resurrection, and the life everlasting. Amen.

Question. What do you chiefly learn in these beliefs?

Answer. First, I learn to believe in God who made me, and all the world. Second, in Jesus, and his redemptive grace. Third, in the Holy Spirit, who sanctifies me, and all who walk in the paths of goodness and light.

Question. Tell me how many commandments there are?

Answer. Ten.

Question. And what are they?

Answer.
1. You shall believe in one God.
2. You shall not make an image of God and worship it.
3. You shall not blaspheme.
4. You shall rest for one day every week.
5. You shall honour your parents.
6. You shall not murder.

7. You shall not commit adultery.
8. You shall not steal.
9. You shall not lie.
10. You shall not covet.

They are summed up by Jesus: "You shall love God with all your heart, soul and mind and you shall love your neighbour as yourself."

Question. What do you learn most from these commandments?

Answer. I learn two things. My duty towards God, and my duty towards my neighbours.

Question. What is your duty towards God?

Answer. My duty towards God is to believe in God and love God, with all my heart, with all my mind, with all my soul, and with all my strength; to worship God, to give God thanks, to put my trust in God, to call upon God, to honour God's Name and God's Word, and to serve God truly all the days of my life.

Question. What is your duty towards your neighbours?

Answer. My duty towards my neighbours is to love them as myself, and to do to all people as I would wish them to do to me. To love, honour, and comfort my parents. To honour and obey those rightfully in authority and acting with integrity. To learn from my governors, teachers, spiritual pastors, and leaders. To order myself in humility and reverently to all others. To hurt nobody by word nor deed. To be true and just in all my dealing. To bear no malice nor hatred in my heart. To keep my hands from stealing, and my tongue from evil speaking, lying, and slandering. To keep my body in temperance, soberness, and chastity. Not to covet nor desire other people's goods, but to learn and labour truly to earn my own living, and to do my duty in all that I do.

Catechist. My sister/brother, know that it is difficult to do these things of yourself, and to walk faithfully in the commandments of God, and to serve God, without a special grace, which you must always learn to call for, by diligent prayer. Let me hear therefore if you can say Jesus's Prayer.

Answer May Love be revered
May unity come
Good will be done
That earth may become our heaven
May we work hard for our daily needs
And may our wrongs be forgiven
As we forgive those
Who have done wrong to us
And may we not fall into temptation
But be delivered from evil
For we believe in Justice, Truth, and Peace

Question. What do you ask God for in this Prayer?

Answer. I desire God, who is the giver of all goodness, to send grace to me, and to all people, that we may worship, serve, and honour God, as we ought to do. And I pray to God to send us all that we need for our souls and bodies; and that God will be merciful unto us and forgive us our sins; and that it will please God to save and defend us in all dangers; and that God will keep us from all sin and wickedness, and from everlasting death. And this I trust God will do out of mercy and goodness.

Question. What is a sacrament?

Answer. It is an outward and visible sign of an inward and spiritual grace given unto us.

Question. What is the outward visible sign or form in Baptism for instance?

Answer. Water, in which the person is baptized.

Question. What is the inward and spiritual grace?

Answer. A death to sin, and new birth to a life of righteousness.

Question. What is required of people to be baptized?

Answer. Repentance, whereby they forsake sin: and faith, whereby they steadfastly believe the promises of God, made to them in that Sacrament.

Question. Why then are infants baptized, when by reason of their tender age they cannot perform them?

Answer. Because promises are made on their behalf.

Question. Why was the Sacrament of Jesus's Supper ordained?

Answer. For the continued remembrance of the sacrifice of the death of Jesus and of the love expressed to us through his life and message.

Question. What is the outward part or sign of Jesus's Supper?

Answer. Food and drink, which Jesus invited us to receive.

Question. What is the inward part, or thing signified?

Answer. The receiving of the life, love, and inspiration of Jesus.

Question. What benefit do we receive from this sacrament?

Answer. The strengthening and refreshing of our souls by the life of Jesus, as our bodies are also, by the food and drink.

Question. What is required of those who come to Jesus's Supper?

Answer. To examine themselves, whether they repent truly of their former sins, and steadfastly intend to lead a new life; have a real faith in God's mercy, with a thankful remembrance of Jesus's death; and a deep love for all people.

BAPTISM AND CONFIRMATION OF AN OLDER CHILD OR ADULT

After the Confession of Holy Communion

Loving God
By whose spirit we are restored and blessed
Impart your sanctifying grace to (-) who is to be numbered among the followers of Jesus, that with a pure heart and open mind s/he may faithfully receive the gift of the Holy Spirit; through Christ, our Saviour.

All. **Amen**.

ALL: GLORIA

Glory to God in the highest,
and peace to his people on earth.
Loving God, heavenly Monarch,
Almighty God and creator, we worship you, we give you thanks,
we praise you for your glory. Loving Jesus Christ,
Cherished Child of God, Loving God, Lamb of God,
you take away the sin of the world:
Have mercy on us; you are seated at the right hand of God:
Receive our prayer.
For you are the Holy One, you are the Saviour,

You are the Most High, Jesus Christ, with the Holy Spirit, in the glory of God the Supreme. Amen.

The Chosen Readings and Psalms

THE BAPTISM

Every rainbow is God's promise of Love that the storm clouds will give way to the sunlight, and the colours of life, will spread once more across our lives.

Gracious God, you want us to know Love, trust Love and show Love. May we surround (-) with Love and protect her/him from evil, that s/he may be filled with the Holy Spirit, and learn to walk with us, in the ways of goodness, justice and truth. Amen

The Questions of Commitment

Do you turn to Christ?

I turn to Christ

Do you repent of your sins?

I repent of my sins

Do you renounce evil?

I renounce evil.

The signing with the cross

I sign you with the cross, the sign of Christ, Love's kiss from heaven. Jesus will walk before you, keeping you safe, following behind, guarding your path, ever at your right hand and at your left, your friend, and your inspiration, ever holding your heart within Love's own.

(-) may you resist the forces of darkness, in the strength and confidence known in Jesus, and learn how to follow faithfully. the paths of compassion and kindness. that lead to life and fulfillment.

The Blessing of the Water

Loving God, thank you for today, for family and friends gathered in celebration. In oftentimes a complicated world, the chance to laugh, love and delight in all that is good.
Thank you for (-). For his/her unique and precious life, given to us for our cherishing.

Thank you for water. For the times we swim and play in it. Thank you for our thirst quenched, our bodies cleansed, our crops watered, and our bodies created from these crystal streams.
Yet, as well as bringing life, this same water teems with danger, taking many lives. It is a potent symbol of life and death, hope and peril.
And today we thank you for Jesus, that good, kind, and loving man, who transformed people's lives, challenging corruption, healing the broken, respecting the children and pointing us all to the hope of building a new society of justice and peace.

Too good for this world, evil came and stole his life, and the tears began to fall, enough to flood the earth, a tsunami of suffering to drown us all. But in the mystery of resurrection, Love, undeterred, irrepressible, rose from that place of death and hopelessness, to inspire us all to play our part in overcoming evil with goodness and despair with hope.

So come Holy Spirit and bless these crystal waters with life and grace abundant, that as they sprinkle (-), she/y may be filled with new life, in all its fulness and shine as a light in this world to bring joy to many.

Questions of Faith

Do you believe and trust in God, the creator of heaven and earth?

I do so believe and trust.

Do you believe and trust in Jesus Christ, whose Love challenges and transforms us?

I do so believe and trust.

Do you believe and trust I the Holy Spirit who inspires and empowers us to live good and loving lives?

I do so believe and trust.

I give you this light because Love's light has filled you.

(-) Let the light of Love shine from within you, guiding your choices, giving hope to others, and leading you to live a good, compassionate, and productive life.

(-) God has received you by baptism into the church. We welcome you as part of the worldwide family of good people. We belong

together and are the living presence of Jesus. We are daughters and sons of the one God. We are inheritors together of Love's promises, and Love's invitation to help change this world for the better

THE CONFIRMATION

As you arise from the waters of baptism, God sends upon you the Holy Spirit to sanctify and empower you.

The world in which we live is far from perfect. It is marred by sin and selfishness. There is a constant struggle between good and evil, and since you are a follower of Jesus, you are called to play your part in resisting what is wrong and being courageous in supporting what is right.

As you enter God's most holy service, ensure that you are such a follower as God would want you to be. Strong, yet gentle, ready always to protect the weak, watchful, and ever willing to volunteer your help, showing respect and courtesy to all, never forgetting that God is Love.

Make it your constant care, to share Love around you wherever you may go and fan into living flame, the smouldering fires of Love in the hearts of those in whom, as yet the spark burns low.

Remember that the followers of Jesus must learn to uproot from their heart, the weeds of selfishness, and must live not for themselves alone, but for the service of others.

For this commandment we have from God, that the one who loves God must love all other people.

Remember, that the power of God, that you receive, symbolised in the placing of my hand on your head, will continually be at work within you to establish you as a good and righteous person.

Strive therefore earnestly that your thoughts, your words, and your works shall be as befits a follower of Jesus, and as one dedicated to Love's service.
All this shall you zealously try to do.

The Questions

Will you then strive to live in the spirit of Love with all other people and earnestly to struggle against sin and selfishness?

I WILL

Will you strive to show in your thoughts your words and your works the power of God which shall be given to you?

I WILL

May the blessing of the Holy Spirit come upon you and may the power of the most high protect you.

I offer myself to be a disciple in Christ's service.

In Christ's most holy name, I welcome you.

THE VENI CREATOR

Come, thou Creator Spirit blest,
And in our souls take up thy rest;
Come with thy grace and
heavenly aid,
To fill the hearts which thou hast made.

Great Paraclete, to thee we cry,
O highest gift of God most high;
O living fount, O fire, O love
And sweet anointing from above.

Thou in thy sevenfold gift art known;
Thee, finger of God's hand, we own;
The promise of the Creator, thou
Who dost the tongue with power endow.

Kindle our senses from above
And make our hearts o'erflow with love;
With patience firm and virtue high
The weakness of our flesh supply.

> Far let us drive our tempting foe
> And thine abiding peace bestow;
> So shall we not, with thee for guide,
> Turn from the path of life aside.
>
> O may thy grace on us bestow
> The Creator and Love to know
> And thee, through endless time confessed,
> Of both eternal Spirit blest.
>
> All glory while the ages run
> Be to the Creator and the One,
> Who gave us life; the same to thee,
> O Holy Ghost, eternally. Amen.

The bishop confirms with the laying on of her/his hand and the anointing.

THE ANOINTING WITH CHRISM

Let your eyes be opened to see all manner of beauty. Let your ears be opened to hear the words of the wise. Let your lips speak words of kindness. Let your hands do good things upon the earth. Let your feet bear you upon the paths that lead to life and let your heart overflow with an unconditional love for all.

My sister/brother now you have received the gift of the Holy Spirit, see to it that you remain pure, clean and steadfast in the pursuit of goodness, as befits the presence of the living God, and the channel of so great a power, and understand that as you keep that channel open, by a useful life, spent in the service of others, so will God's life, that is within you, shine forth with ever greater glory

Our help is in the name of God

Who has made heaven and earth.

Blessed are the pure in heart

For they shall see God.

Trust in God forever

For God is our rock of ages.

God be with you and with your spirit

THE COMMUNION CONTINUES

EQUAL MARRIAGE LITURGIES

In the name of Love; creative, redemptive and life giving.

May God's love and peace and happiness be with you.
or
May love and peace and happiness fill you and surround you.

Introduction

God is love, and those who live in love live in God and God lives in them.

Select from:

Love is a trembling happiness.

I love you ever and ever and without reserve. The more I have known you the more I have loved.

When I see you, then I am well. If you open your eyes, my body is young again. If you speak, then I am strong again.

Love is the heart's immortal thirst to be completely known and all forgiven.

Where, O where do I begin, to tell you how much I love you; how much you've changed my life; how much I long to be with you?

I never realised what love was - until I met you.

I want only to walk beside you; to pass through this world beside you; to fulfil my destiny beside you.

You are the rock upon which I want to build my life, my future and my all.

Where love beckons........follow.

The Introduction

You stand together on the threshold of a myriad of dreams and hopes; for love has brought you, bright eyed and eager, to this place.

Today, you enter the most sacred place within the land of love. A garden reserved for those who have found their heart's delight and their soul's awakening.

When two people understand each other in their inmost hearts their words are sweet and strong like the fragrance of orchids.

God our Creator, you have taught us, that love is the most beautiful experience of our lives. Grant to (-) such love towards one another, that they

may embrace in love until their lives' end.
Through Jesus, Amen.

God of love, we thank you for love. The love which found us when we were alone, warmed us when we were cold, soothed us when hurting and healed us when broken. Thank you for the love which has breathed new life within us, shone new light upon us and graced each day with hope. Thank you for this love made known to (-) through each other, which this day we celebrate and honour and commit unto you, the bestower and sustainer of all that is good, Amen.

We have come together in the presence of God to witness the marriage of (-), to ask for blessing upon them, and to share in their happiness.

Or

We have come together to witness the marriage of (-). We are their friends and their family. We value them and are with them today as they set out on this great adventure of marriage.

Or

We have gathered today to celebrate the love of (-), to ask God's blessing upon them and give them our blessing and surround them with our love and support.

Or

We have met today to bless the marriage of (-), to be thankful for the love they know and share together and to witness the promises they will make to one another.

(If the marriage ceremony is after a registry office wedding)

(-) completed the legal formalities for marriage/were legally married, -, at the registry office/by the registrar, - yesterday/this morning/on the - of - (date), but for them this is - their true wedding/the occasion they regard as their real marriage/ what is necessary to make their marriage complete, when surrounded by those they love, they make their vows to one another and receive - God's blessing/our blessing.

Then select from the following paragraphs:

(-) come from different families, they are different people, they have walked different paths. But in a mysterious way, all the steps they have taken have led them to the wonder of this moment.

Love from their parents and grandparents, from their brothers and sisters and from their family and friends; this love, richly, fully, freely given has helped make them what they are today and enabled them to offer the gift of their unique lives to each other.

Today we celebrate the discovery and the nurturing of their special love for each other and the way it has further enriched their lives and we look forward with them to all the promise that the future holds.

Marriage is the promise of hope between two people who love each other, who trust that love, who honour one another as individuals and who wish to share their future together.

It enables two separate people to share their desires, longings, dreams and memories, their joys and their laughter and to help each other through the times of uncertainty. It provides the encouragement to risk more and thus to gain more.

When we love, we see things other people cannot. We see beneath the surface and observe that which others may not. To see with loving eyes is to know an inner beauty, and to be loved is to be seen and known as we are known to no other.

When we love we are loved and when we are loved we love. Love gives birth to love and hope and trust and joy. Love sets us free to be ourselves. Love gives us wings with which to fly. Love is the sunlight which warms our hearts and lives. It is this beautiful love which (-) have discovered, which has changed their lives, which has brought them to this moment.

In marriage, two people embark upon a journey that has no ending only an infinite number of beginnings. They face the mystery of the future and all that awaits them. The years will change them, but as a family is bonded eternally together, parent to child, sister to brother, so two people in marriage. Love allows for no separation.

As such the pathways of love are exacting as well as bountiful. This day history shall record the joining together of two lives, two families, two groups of friends. There is nothing in all the delights and deceits of this world that can ever erase the fact that this bond will have been made.

Even if in the future the law, shall, out of necessity, name the bond as broken, the fact is forever lodged, that those united this day were joined. They may become estranged as does happen, but as a part of each other's history, they shall forever remain.

Furthermore, those who are blessed by love's greatest miracle and so bear children into this world, must know that the coloured threads of two families are woven into their creation and their lives. By their birth an irrevocable union has been made. However far apart the parents may travel from each other, they will always meet again at the bridge of their children's lives.

As such, those bonded in love do well to heed the wisdom of the ages: that they tend to one another as to no other, that there is no erasing of the covenant made in marriage and through birth, and that there is no relationship on earth comparable to the one shared with your wedded partner.

Those who have already been married bear in their hearts the pain they have known and the wisdom they have gained through all that has been. Today, knowing from whence they have come and what is theirs to do, they set their face towards a new path and a new future.

(Names of any children from past relationships/ Names of any children from the present relationship) is/are a supremely important part of the future and (-) love her/him/them and will always cherish her/him/them and be there for her/him/them.

There are few things that can so damage a soul as a love lost or broken. For someone to suffer that shattering, to collect the broken shards of their life and to restore themselves sufficiently to respond to love's sweet presence is a marvellous thing.

Generous life affords to every one of us so many chances, so much mercy and so much hope. That hope, effervescent within us, is the keeper of our souls. How grateful are (-), that through everything and despite everything they have found one another. In one another, their treasure has at last been discovered and their dreams fulfilled.

In marriage, you are joined together.

Two people discover every contour of their partner's soul and being and every emotion is available to be experienced. They may well love, hate, like, despise, be proud of and ashamed of each other. They may have dreams fulfilled and dashed, be excited and bored, stretched and limited, set free and imprisoned, rage, laugh, weep and dance, and all with the one they love, because this is love.

This is not the sentimental, transitory, and oftentimes fickle love of early passion, of fiction and of fantasy.

True love is often a messy, complicated happening, with its struggles, heartaches, confusions and uncertainties; but what is known by those who have faced all, endured all and stood the test of time, is that the jewel beyond price, the fulfilment beyond description, the security beyond knowledge is found by those who have offered to each other an unconditional love, who have been willing to cope with and face anything and everything together, and who are thus able to journey on as closest friends.

In a few moments we shall be present as this great covenant of love is enacted before us. (-) will affirm their choice and desire to enter the hallowed realm of marriage. They will speak their solemn words of promise and commitment. A new family will be born in our midst and a profound happiness will bless us all.

In a few moments we shall witness (-) promises, we shall share with them their happiness as a newly married couple and all their hopes for the future.

HERE INSERT A SELECTION OF CHOSEN READINGS, RELIGIOUS/SECULAR – POETRY/PROSE

THE MARRIAGE

Select from the following:

The Scriptures teach us that marriage is a generous gift of God, a holy mystery in which two people weave the fabric of their lives together.

Marriage is given, that they may comfort and help each other, living faithfully together in need and in plenty, in sorrow and in joy. It is given, that with delight and tenderness they may know each other in love, and, through the joy of their bodily union, may strengthen the union of their hearts and lives.

Marriage expresses the strength of love and devotion enjoyed by two people whose lives have become woven together. Their appreciation of one another and the confidence they have in their relationship bring them to this important step. Our horizons always contain mystery, but marriage enables our journey onwards to be warmed and enriched by the presence of another, in whom we invest our trust, our hope, our life.

(-) you believe in a relationship based on openness, in which each will love, honour, and treasure the other, remaining devoted companions for all your days. Listening and laughing, caring and sharing, you wish to live your lives to the full, enabling one another through encouragement and sensitive words.

Marriage enables two people to discover each other as never before; to journey towards the centre of each other's soul, mind, heart, and body; to be confronted by places of woundedness; to wound and be wounded, just as to discover rich sources of life, to create and be recreated.

There exist within marriage some of our greatest emotional and spiritual possibilities. We marry not only to be loved and feel secure, to come home to our loved one and have our needs met; we marry also to enhance our capacity to love, to nurture, to give and forgive, to heal and to inspire.

When we love we exercise our choice. Being quite capable of living without each other, two people yet choose to live together; and in that choosing, to entertain the hope of something more wonderful being created through the weaving of the coloured threads of their lives.

When you love someone, you do not feel love for them all the time, in the same way, from moment to moment. We have so little faith in the ebb and flow of life, of love, of relationships. We leap at the flow of the tide and resist, in terror, its ebb. We are afraid it will never return. We insist on permanency, on duration, on continuity; when the only continuity possible, in life, as in love, is in growth, in fluidity - in freedom, in the sense that dancers are free, barely touching as they pass, but partners in the same pattern.

The only real security in a relationship, is not in owning or possessing, not in demanding or expecting, not looking back to what was in nostalgia, nor forward to what might be in dread or anticipation but living in the present moment.

Relationships are like islands, joined yet interrupted by the sea, continually visited, and yet also abandoned by the tides.

A marriage is not a prison but a wide open space; not a set of chains but a path to freedom.

Maintaining that liberty is the essence of love. It will be witness to each partner's choices and changes, the mistakes, and the glory. It can cause the heart to bleed and the soul to despair but such suffering, blended with joy, and fermented over the years, creates love's vintage wine that brings delight.

A good family watches with each other through all the changing scenes of life and holds within its embrace the bruises and the benefits of its loved ones. In marriage a new family is born. Your vows will commission you, to be so devoted in your love, that all the follies of this world and of each other will not have the power to separate you.

(-) this day you will marry your friend, the one you laugh with, live for, dream with, love. As your marriage brings new meaning to love, so your love will bring new meaning to life. From this day forward, let it be one promise, one dream, one love.

This is the way of life which (-) are now to begin. They will each give their consent to the other; they will join hands and exchange solemn vows, and in token of this they will give and receive a ring.

Does anyone present know of any lawful reason why (-) should not be joined in holy matrimony? If so, speak now or forever hold your peace.

THE QUESTIONS OF CONSENT

N, will you take N to be your spouse/wife/husband? Will you love her/him, comfort her/him, honour and protect her/him, and, forsaking all others (Or: placing her/him above all others), be faithful (Or: be open and honest) to her/him as long as you both shall live?

Or

Wilt thou have this woman/man to thy wedded spouse/wife/husband, to live together after God`s ordinance in the holy estate of matrimony? Wilt thou love her/him, comfort her/him, honour and keep her/him in sickness and in health and, forsaking all others, keep thee only unto her/him, so long as ye both shall live?

I wilt or I will.

Or

N, will you take N to be your spouse/wife/husband? Will you journey beside her/him from this day on? Will hers/his be the hand you hold, the heart you adore, the soul you honour and will you give her/him the freedom and the security within which s/he can thrive and flourish.

I WILL

Or

N, will you cherish N's life and his/her destiny? Will you value the gift of his/her love and his/her commitment to you? Will you always be mindful of the great responsibility you assume today for his/her wellbeing and will you always tend to him/her as to no other.

I WILL

Or

N, will you love N unconditionally, whatever life may bring. Will you sleep beside him/her, walk beside him/her, laugh with him/her and cry with him/her? Will you love him/her with tenderness and with truth and take care to guard this precious love you share? Will you be there for him/her at the turning of the road and the rising of the path? Will you be his/hers from this day to the setting of your lives?

I WILL

∎∎

Asked of both:

Who accompanies this woman/man as s/he marries this woman/man?

I/we do

Said to all the parents/guardians:

You brought (-) into the world. Through the tender years, you nursed them, loved them, and watched over them. Your hearts and your homes have been their nourishment and as so often in the past they look today for your favour. Do you offer your son/s/daughter/s your blessing for their marriage?

We do.

Said to the guests:

Will you, their friends, and their family support them and be there for them in the days to come. Will you be generous in your care, thoughtful in your concern and imaginative in your friendship?

We will

I invite you now to join your hands as you exchange your vows. The hand offered by each of you is a part of yourself. Cherish this touch, for you touch not only your own life, but also that of another precious person. Be ever sensitive to them, to their hopes and their dreams, and help make their dreams come true.

THE MARRIAGE VOWS

Select from:

Today I see you as if for the first time. For as much as I know you so well, you are new to me. Today you become my beloved partner in marriage. This is a beginning and a continuing; a whole new world and one that has already graced our lives.

Or

I, N, take you, N, to be my spouse/wife/husband: to have and to hold, from this day forward; for better, for worse; for richer, for poorer; in sickness and in health; to love and to cherish, till death us do part; according to God's holy law; and this is my solemn vow.

Or

I N, take thee N, to be my wedded spouse/wife/husband, to have and to hold from this day forward for better for worse, for richer for poorer, in sickness and in health, to love and to cherish, till death us do part, according to God`s holy ordinance, and thereto I pledge thee my troth

Or

Today, I give myself to you as your spouse/wife/husband: all that I am, and all that I have; and I receive, the precious gift of you, as my beloved spouse/wife/husband. For all the days of my life, I will treasure you, I will cherish you and I will be utterly devoted to you, through the laughter and the tears, through the darkness and the light, I will be your everlasting love, your constant companion, your closest friend, pledging to you my deepest   commitment And this is my solemn vow.

Or

Day by day I promise
to love and to honour you
to treasure you and to respect you
to walk with you side by side
in joy and sorrow

Day by day I promise
to hold you in my arms
to grow with you in truth
to laugh with you, to cry with you
to be with you
and to love you with all that I am and all that I shall become

This I promise you from the depth of my heart, my mind, and my soul - for all our lives together.

OR

From this day on I choose you my beloved N, to be my spouse/wife/husband
To live with you and laugh with you.
To stand by your side and sleep in your arms.
To be joy to your heart and food to your soul
To be your constant companion and closest friend.
To love you and bring out the best in you always.
And to be the best that I can be, for you.

Or

To you I give my heart,
I give my soul,
I give my very self.
Into your hands I place
my hopes and dreams,
my strength and weakness.
To you I give my trust, my highest
and my best.
To you and only you will I be for ever true.

Or

No one has touched my life like you.
No one can compare with you,
No one has made my heart leap and my soul
dance,
nor set my mind alight with joy.
In your presence I have found my rest, my home,
myself.
In your arms I have known such peace.
Today I give myself to you.
I am yours and ever shall it be.

Or

On this momentous day,
it is my choice, my will, and my delight,
to wed you my beloved N.
Our love has changed my life, no more the search.
I have found you, my heart's desire,

and nothing will ever take me from your side,
You are my all and my only,
and with you shall I travel to my rest.

Or

I want to spend the rest of my life with you, only you.
I want to fall asleep each night with you by my side.
I want to tell you what fills my soul.
I want to love you for ever and for always.

I want you to be the father/mother of my child.
I want you to be my lifelong friend and lover.
I want you to awaken my life with your love.

I want us to fill the coming years with wonderful memories.
I want us to face everything together.
I want you. I want you and me. I want us.

Or

I love you
I love you unconditionally
I will love you whatever tomorrow brings
I will love you however much you change
My love is like a rock upon which you can build your life
My love is constant, certain, and committed
My love will never waver, nor run dry
I declare that my lifelong vow

is to so love you, day by day and year by year
that I become your greatest blessing,
and your richest source of happiness.

Or

You are so beautiful/handsome to me,
You are my life, my light, my hope, my joy.
You are my food, my drink, my music, and my song,
You are my warmth, my shelter, my passion, and my rest.
You are my world.

And I am yours.
Your friend, your lover, and your soul mate.
So let the whole world hear and know
that I love you
and I vow that my love will bring you joy.

THE GIVING OF THE RING/S

You have brought one/two ring/s in recognition of your vows.

Or

You have brought one/two ring/s as a sign of your marriage.

A circle is the symbol of the sun and the earth and the universe. It represents wholeness and peace and a love which never ever ends.

Or

In the turning of the earth and the cycle of the seasons, in the dance of sun, moon and stars, on the great wheel of life which knows of no end nor even its beginning; so the circle of love encompasses all, promises all, gives birth to all and protects all.

Or

Heavenly God, by your blessing, let these rings be to (-) a symbol of unending love and faithfulness, to remind them of the vow and covenant which they have made this day. Amen.

Then

Give them now, that they may always remind you of how much you are in love today, the day you commit and entrust yourselves to each other for all eternity.

Then

I give you this ring, as a sign of our marriage. With my body I honour you, all that I am I give to you, and all that I have I share with you, within the love of God.

Or

I give you this ring, as a symbol of our marriage. May we be encircled by each other's love, always close to each other, always secure in each other's care.

Or

Whenever you hold this ring know that I shall always come home to you, and my heart will be brimming over with love for you.

Or

With this ring I thee wed, with my body I thee honour, and all my worldly goods with thee I share. In the name of the Creator, the Redeemer, and the Sanctifier

Or

This ring is a symbol of all that I am. Receive and treasure it as a pledge of the love I have for you; and wear it to protect you whenever we are apart. From this day forward we are as one.

Or

I give you this ring: because I love you, because I always want to be with you, because I place my life in your hands, because I will hold you for ever.

Or

I give you this ring, as a sign that I have chosen
you above all others to share life's journey
May we be encircled by each other's love all the
days of our lives.

Or

I bind thee to me,
As I to thee.
Golden mantle of my love,
Shining symbol of my eternal devotion.

Or

I claim you this day as my own.
Wear this emblem of our love with pride.
Let all who see it know,
That with thee I shall for ever abide.

THE DECLARATION OF MARRIAGE

In the presence of God, and before their families
and friends, (-) have made their marriage vows to
each other. They have declared their marriage by
the joining of hands and by the giving and
receiving of a ring. I therefore proclaim that they
are now married, in the sight of God.

Or

Inasmuch as (-) have grown in knowledge and love for one another, and because they have agreed in their desire to go forward in their life together, seeking an even richer and deeper relationship, and because they have pledged to meet sorrow and joy as one family, it gives me great pleasure to now pronounce that they are united in marriage.

Or

Here in our presence intimate words have been spoken, dreams unfurled, hopes set free. It has been our privilege to hear, to bear witness and to share these timeless moments. A love born in times past has today known its blossoming and therefore it is my joyful task to now announce that (-) are married.

Or

Here before us (-) have embarked upon a unique journey. Their love will take them beyond the borders, across unknown continents, to whole new worlds beyond; but today we are with them, beside them, loving them, wishing them their highest dreams, bidding them safely on their way; for now (-) are a married couple.

Or

Something remarkable has taken place.
Two lives, once separate, have been joined.
In the giving, and the promising, in the hoping and the pledging, a new world has been born, a new horizon glimpsed, a new path found, a new course set. (-) are now united in marriage.

Or

We have heard with our ears and seen with our eyes. Our hearts have been moved and our spirits stirred. We have been witnesses to an eternal pledge, a lifelong commitment, a timeless hope. Today in our presence, (-) have become a married couple.

You may kiss

That which God has joined together, let no other seek to divide.

Or

That which love has brought together, let no other try to part.

(Optional additional ceremonies)

THE CANDLE LIGHTING CEREMONY

Your love burns today as a flame within your hearts. So, join now those burning hearts and light up a torch of love.

The couple light individual candles and with them light a central larger candle

Guard well this flickering light of love, that burning bright through happy days and darkest nights, it may for ever provide your warmth, your direction, and your hope.

THE SHARING OF WINE CEREMONY

You have shared together the fruits of love and your times together have been blessed.
Drink now this rich wine, fruit of the earth, symbol of life, of creation, of passion and of love.

Bride and groom sip wine from the same silver vessel.

May the power of love as strong wine ever flow within your veins and may the taste of the grape ever remind you of this moment when your mouths, as your lives, were burning with the joy of each other.

THE SHARING OF HONEY CEREMONY

You have tasted the sweetness of love, intense and profound. Refresh each other now with the touch of honey upon your lips.

The couple in turn collect a tiny amount of honey with a silver spoon from a silver vessel and give it to each other.

May the touch of your lips, as your lives, be delicate and sweet, and as a thousand bees upon a thousand flowers have gathered this rich nectar may the exercise of your love be as constant and as colourful all your days.

THE BLESSING OF THE COUPLE

God the Creator, God the Redeemer, God the Sanctifier, bless, preserve, and keep you; God mercifully grant you the riches of Love's grace, that you may please God both in body and soul, and living together in faith and love, may receive the blessings of eternal life. **Amen.**

OR

May God bless you and watch over you, God make Love's face shine upon you and be gracious to you,

God look kindly on you and give you peace; and the blessing of the Creator, the Redeemer, and the Sanctifier be with you and fill your hearts and fill your home now and for evermore. Amen.

Or

Now may you feel no rain, FOR EACH OF YOU WILL BE SHELTER TO THE OTHER.
Now may you feel no cold, FOR EACH OF YOU WILL BE WARMTH TO THE OTHER. Now may there be no more loneliness, FOR EACH OF YOU WILL BE COMPANION TO THE OTHER.
Now you are two bodies, BUT THERE IS ONLY ONE LIFE BEFORE YOU, AND MAY THAT LIFE AND ALL YOUR DAYS BE GOOD AND LONG UPON THIS GLORIOUS EARTH.

Or

May you know such love together; may you be sunlight for each other's growth, strength for each other's weakness, care for each other's pain, laughter for each other's success and in the unfolding of your lives may you become each other's greatest blessing.

Or

May you become the greatest friends, the most tender lovers, the most devoted companions, the most attentive listeners, the happiest playmates and the securest of couples.

Or

May nothing in all of creation ever separate you from each other. May you stand strong against the dangers of tomorrow and stand tall in facing the challenges ahead. May your hope and trust in one another never fail and if damaged or under threat, may you discover unlimited resources of patience and forgiveness.

May you learn to cope with every emotion, all situations, the darkness and the light, the terrors of hell and the fruits of paradise; but through all, may the years bear witness to your love, which having passed the test of time may deliver you into the last days, hearts entwined, older, wiser, but so much more in love than in these headier days of your beginning.

To such a journey, such an adventure, such a voyage of discovery we your family and friends commend you this day in greatest joy.

Or

Let not a day pass without you expressing your love, reaffirming your devotion, nourishing one other. You hold within your marriage all that is precious, all that is good; value it among all things most highly and know that it is your source of life and happiness, and may that happiness be abundant for all the years to come.

THE SIGNING

The legal signing may have already been carried out or will be later, however the couple may wish there to be an act of signing, when they, and their witnesses, sign the cleric's register, and a special document, that they will keep. If this is not the legal signing, then the document can be formatted as desired, and the couple can choose to have more than two witnesses should they wish.

PRAYERS AND READINGS

Select from

We rejoice today in the marriage of (-). We celebrate the love that brought them to this day. With love that deepens through many years, may they know its meaning and its mystery.

May your house be a place of happiness for all who enter it, a place for growing, and a place for laughter. And when shadows and darkness fall within its rooms, may it still be a place of hope and strength for all who may enter. may no person be alien to your compassion. may your family be the family of all humankind. And may you be blessed with a lifetime of joy.

At this moment rich with meaning, hope and promise, let us pray that the love that has brought you together may continue to grow and enrich your lives.

No marriage is perfect for no one is perfect. So may God give you unrelenting patience to accept each other's faults and failings and to learn to forgive one another fully and freely.

Express your thoughts and emotions, speak openly and honestly, listen to, encourage, and respect one another. Protect the love you share and strive to be a living example of the beautiful relationship that is possible between two people.

All loving God, giver of life and love, bless (-), whom you have joined in marriage. Grant them wisdom and devotion in their life together, that each may be to the other a strength in need, a comfort in sorrow, and a companion in joy. So unite their wills in your will, and their spirits in your spirit, that they live and grow together in love and peace all the days of their life. Amen.

Eternal, true, and loving God, in holy marriage you make your people one. May (-)'s life together witness to your love in this troubled world; may their unity overcome division, forgiveness heal injury and joy triumph over sorrow. Amen.

Gracious God, we pray that through their marriage, (-) may know you more clearly, love you more dearly and follow you more nearly, day by day. Amen.

Saviour Jesus, who shared at Nazareth the life of an earthly home; grant that your spirit may fill (-)'s home, so that they bring forth the fruit of love and joy and peace and are able to minister to others as you have ministered to them. (Bless them in the gift and care of children, who surrounded by security and goodness, may grow up with confidence and hope.) Amen.

Make us instruments of your peace. Where there is hatred, let us sow love; where there is injury, pardon; where there is doubt, faith; where there is despair, hope; where there is darkness, light, and where there is sadness, joy. O Divine Love, grant that we may not so much seek to be consoled as to console; to be understood as to understand, to be loved as to love; for it is in giving that we receive; it is in pardoning that we are pardoned, and it is in dying that we are born to eternal life. Amen

Eternal God, may (-) understand, accept, and forgive each other. As they build their home together, we pray that it may be bright with the laughter of many friends. May your spirit help it to be a haven from the tensions of our times, a source of strength and security, and by your grace may it be the one place in the whole world where they love to be. Amen.

O God, you created the universe and made us in your own likeness. You gave us the constant companionship of another to love, so that they should no longer be two, but one, and you teach us that what you have united should not be divided.

Look with love upon this couple, joined in marriage. They ask for your blessing. Give them the grace of love and peace. May they follow the example of good and holy people. Keep them true to your commandments and faithful in marriage and let them be living examples of Christian life that they may they be witnesses of Love's way to others.

Bless them with children and help them to be good parents. May they live to see their children's children, and, after a happy old age, grant them fullness of life in the paradise of heaven.
Amen

ALTERNATIVE THOUGHTS/PRAYERS:

We hope only good things for you.
We dream only good things for you.
We pray only good things for you.

Walk peacefully.
Dance joyously.
Love passionately.
Kiss tenderly.
Live fully and so may it only be.

How we long for your happiness.
Treasure one another as life's greatest gift.
Cherish the days you share,
The warm moments of your waking and sleeping,
The grind and marvel of your years side by side.
The intoxicating liquor of love with its pain and its passion.
Its loving and its hating.
Cherish all this.
It is but for a tiny moment
upon life's ever turning wheel.

Caress the day you found each other.
Worship the ground upon which you stood.
Hallowed is the place of your becoming,
Hallowed is your touch that turns all to good.

Embrace the seconds of your talking,
Exalt the moments that you share,
Awesome is the ease which leaves predicting,
Awesome is the grace that finds us bare.

Absolve the torment of your failings,
Sanctify the rare quest to forgive
Divine is the freedom that means releasing
Divine is the love you pledge to live.

Fear not the morrow; alone you are no more.
Held in another's care.
The world awaits your coming.

Your destiny is a mystery, mischievously hiding.
Discover well its secrets and may you be surprised
By the excellence of love

When you are afraid, turn to each other.
When life is cruel, find refuge in each other.
When your horizons are vast, forget not each other.
When your hearts are full, be generous with each other.
And when many years have passed, be glad.
For in remaining true to one another,
You will have journeyed to the well of happiness
In each other's soul.

Aspire to the highest love.
Give and never count the cost.
Struggle and never heed the wounds.
Labour and never seek for any reward,
Save that of knowing that you do love's bidding.

Today you are in love. Tomorrow you must love.
Love that values the other and seeks only their best.
Love that understands frailty and failure and is eager to forgive.
Love that copes with strange habits and surprising idiosyncrasies.
Love that swallows hard and laughs generously

Love that protects by foregoing beguiling pleasures.
Love that knows the time to weep and the time to smile.
Love that knows the mystery and privilege of crossing from the boundary of self to the other through their open and trusting heart.
Love that knows how to walk with humble step amidst the treasures of the beloved's soul.

PRAYER FOR EVERYONE TO SAY IF THEY WISH

May Love be revered
May unity come
Good will be done
That earth may become our heaven
May we work hard for our daily needs
And may our wrongs be forgiven
As we forgive those
Who have done wrong to us
And may we not fall into temptation
But be delivered from evil
For we believe in Justice, Truth, and Peace

FINAL BLESSINGS

God the Holy Trinity, make you strong in faith and love, defend you on every side, and guide you in truth and peace; and the blessing of the all loving God, the Creator, the Redeemer and the Sanctifier, be with you and those whom you love and remain with you always. Amen.

Or

May the road rise up to meet you, May the wind be always at your back, May the sun shine warm upon your face, and the rains fall soft upon your fields, and wherever you travel, may the Divine One hold you and protect you in the palm of Love's hand.
Amen.

Or

Deep peace of the running waves to you, Deep peace of the flowing air to you, Deep peace of the quiet earth to you, Deep peace of the gentle night to you, Deep peace of the shining stars to you, Deep peace of the bearers of peace to you, Peace, peace, peace. Amen.

Or

May the raindrops fall lightly on your brows; may the soft winds freshen your spirits: may the sunshine brighten your hearts; may the burdens of each day rest lightly upon you, and may God enfold you in the mantle of Love. Amen.

Or

May love be your blessing, May happiness be your gift, May peace and contentment be your reward, May hope overflow from within you. And may the God of all tenderness and care, walk beside you and protect you through the journey of your days and of your years.
Amen.

Or

May the sun bring you new energies by day.
MAY THE MOON SOFTLY RESTORE YOU BY NIGHT.
May the rain wash away any worries you may have.
AND THE BREEZE BLOW NEW STRENGTH INTO YOUR BEING.
And then all the days of your life
MAY YOU WALK GENTLY THROUGH THE WORLD AND KNOW ITS BEAUTY.

Or

May the emotions of these moments be constant visitors to your hearts.
May the warmth, smiles and laughter of your guests be heard and felt across the coming years.
May the intense beauty of these hours last for your lifetime together

And may you never forget the rich love that is yours today.

CONCLUDING WORDS

Now, as this ceremony closes, may love and laughter, hope and happiness fill the air and flow from heart to heart. May old friendships be strengthened - new friendships born and in the interweaving of your lives may love surround (-) on this their wedding day and for all their days to come.

Or

A wedding is a remarkable and beautiful occasion. We have been touched, moved, and inspired today. Words about love, promises made in love, the innocence of (-)'s love; all these things have refreshed us, challenged us, reminded us. Nothing can compare with love. So, as we turn from this ceremony to the excitement of the reception to follow, may our words and our conversations be full of love to bless (-) on this their happy day.

Or

The wedding is not over, it has just begun. Not once and forever, but again and again, shall the mystery of two people, together and in love, move them, and us, and touch the world. For marriage is not something said and done, but a promise whose fulfillment will grace all the years ahead.

Or

Arise, and go with your loved one. See! Your winter is past; the frosts of your loneliness are over and gone. God's flowers appear where you tread; the season of singing has come, and the cooing of doves is heard in your land. Go then and dance to the sweet melodies of love.

Or

A symphony of words draws to its end. The last strains of love's orchestra fill the air. Love is all around us and so it should be on this most profound of days. The wedding feast bids us welcome. Fine food and wine will carry us away to yet more happy hours and so let us with radiant smiles and happiest hearts greet (-).

Or

The wedding service is almost over. It only leaves me to wish (-) so much love and happiness for today and for a lifetime and to ask you all to make this the most unforgettable and wonderful day of their lives as you join them in celebrating their love, their hopes and their marriage.

FUNERALS

Most of the funeral, if the family wish, should be about the bereaved. The role of the minister is to spend extended quality time with the family, asking comprehensive questions about the person's life, from birth to death, and gaining as much information as possible about their loved one.

A high quality of pastoral care is required, and a well-honed ability needed, to sensitively glean this vital information, in such a way, that the funeral visit itself, can be a healing, comforting, and uplifting time, awakening beautiful memories, and drawing the bereaved close.

The family's choices take precedence in all matters, so that they decide/approve the style of service, the music, the contributors, the poetry and readings, the presence or absence of religious material and the attire of the minister/celebrant.

Generally, as most of the service is personal and about the bereaved, any additional material will be minimal and only used to cushion and comfort, where appropriate.

The following material can be considered, as a framework for a service.

Opening Music

Opening prayer of Comfort and Consolation

O God of gentle love
You first brought (-) to birth
And we know it was surrounded
By the love of family and friends
That s/he lived happily and well
And we believe
It was into the arms of love that s/he died
In all our grief and pain
Draw close we pray
Embrace us with your care
And fill our aching hearts
With the promise of new life
That (-), as all of our loved ones, passed over
Remains ever with us
Just a breath away
In the paradise beyond
Through Jesus, our comforter, Amen

Reading/Poem

Family Tributes

Music

Memories (When you speak at length and personally about the bereaved)

Music

Prayers

Additional prayers here may not be necessary.

Prayers of Love and Farewell

It is important to learn the basic structure of these words, so that you can adapt them, personalise them and improvise, as may be appropriate to make the service, and especially this critical part of it, personal and comforting.

Beloved (-)
How we have loved you, respected you and appreciated you.
We want to say 'thank you' though such a word could never be enough.
You have been the foundation upon which we have built our lives. You have brought delight to our days and surrounded us with love.
Your heart has been ever busy, in a myriad of special moments, enriching, enhancing, and blessing us, your cherished family and friends.
Your words and ways have so finely interlaced our days.
And now this sacred vessel of your spirit
Once so busy about life
Lies still before us
It is a body for which you have no further use

With which you so bravely contended in the final days of your weakening
Which we have adorned with flowers
And surrounded with our love and affection
And which we now prepare to have cremated
Earth to earth
Ashes to ashes
Dust to death
And we do so
In the love of Jesus
Who died and who rose again
To give us hope and the promise of new life
And so, this day, we release your lovely spirit
To the wide blue expanse of the sky
To the sun's warmth and the wind's breath
To the dance of the stars and the planets
(-) go safely, across the rainbow bridge of all of our dreams
With the promise of resurrection
Into the safe keeping of God
And the wonders of paradise
And to loved ones, waiting upon that golden shore
And oh, how we will miss you
Never to forget you
Ever to talk of you
And one day
To be together with you again
And until then
Our love remains always with you

The family will have chosen here whether the curtains close or stay open etc and whether music plays or not

Then words akin to:

I'd love the memory of me to be a happy one
I'd love to leave an afterglow of smiles when my life is done
I'd love to leave an echo
Whispering softly down the ways
Of all the bright and happy times that truly blessed our days
And I'd like the tears of those who grieve
To dry before the sun of all these lovely memories
Now my life is done

Closing Blessing of Life and Hope

We are not going to leave (-) here, it could never be, nor any of our loved ones.
(-) is ever with you, cherished deep in your hearts. You can hear her/his voice still, close your eyes and see her/his face. You know what s/he would say in any situation. S/he will always be at your side, as you face each twist and turn of the journey ahead, so journey on in hope and strength to the new horizons that await.

And in these hurting days, comfort one another, and wipe each other's tears away, and may we all be held safe, in the palm of God's loving hands. Amen

DIACONAL ORDINATION

God be with you.

And also with you.

CONFESSION and ABSOLUTION

(Here we pause to reflect silently on the ways in which we are unaligned and culpable as individuals and as communities.)

Loving God, we acknowledge our wrongdoing, misdeeds, and culpability. We are truly sorry for our part in damaging ourselves, others and creation and intend to do our best to put things right, make amends and live anew.

May God who is Creator, Redeemer and Sanctifier, bless, preserve and sanctify us, may the divine look kindly upon us and be gracious to us; may Love absolve us from all our sins and grant us the grace and comfort of the Holy Spirit.

Amen.

THE COLLECT

Loving God, by whose spirit we are restored and blessed, impart your sanctifying grace to (-) who is to be numbered among the deacons of your church, that with a pure heart and open mind s/he may faithfully receive the gift of the Holy Spirit; through Christ, our Saviour.

Amen.

GLORIA

Glory to God in the highest,
and peace to his people on earth.
Loving God, heavenly Monarch,
Almighty God and creator, we worship you, we give you thanks,
we praise you for your glory. Loving Jesus Christ, Cherished Child of God, Loving God, Lamb of God, you take away the sin of the world:
Have mercy on us; you are seated at the right hand of God:
Receive our prayer.
For you are the Holy One, you are the Saviour,
You are the Most High, Jesus Christ, with the Holy Spirit, in the glory of God the Supreme.
Amen.

THE FIRST READING

Psalm

SECOND READING

Presenter: I ask that you now ordain this candidate here present to the order of the diaconate.

Bishop. Do you know her/him to be worthy?

As far as human frailty allows me to judge, I do both know and attest that s/he is worthy of the charge of this office.

Bishop. Thanks be to God.

If anyone has any reason to believe that this ordination should not proceed, and that this person should not be ordained as a deacon, then let them boldly come forward and present their reasons. However, let them first consider their own integrity and motivation.

Then will those gathered here today, support (-) in her/his ministry?

We will.

Bishop:

You are being raised to the order of the diaconate. God has given an example for you to follow.

As a deacon you will serve Jesus, who was known among his disciples as the one who served others.

Do the will of God generously. Serve God and all people with love and joy.

Like those the apostles chose for works of charity, you should be a good person, filled with wisdom and the Holy Spirit. Show before God and all people that you are a truly like Jesus, and a minister of God's mysteries, a person firmly rooted in faith and abiding in Love.

Acknowledge your faults and remember that no one in the sight of God is blameless or without sin; Christ renews you with a grace and an unending love that never wavers. God has called you by name and you have answered that call; today you will receive the gift of the Holy Spirit through the laying on of hands, you will be raised to the sacred order of the diaconate, and you will begin a new chapter of your life in Christ.

Never turn away from the hope that the Gospel offers; you must not only listen to God's word but live it and preach it. Hold the mystery of faith with a clear conscience. Express in action what you proclaim by word of mouth, so that good people, brought to life by the Spirit, will be liberated into fullness of life. Then finally, on the last day, you will hear Love say:

"Well done, good and faithful friend, enter into the joy of heaven."

Bishop:

Before you are ordained a deacon, you must declare before the people your intention to undertake this office. Are you willing to be ordained for the Church's ministry by the laying on of hands and the gift of the Holy Spirit?

CANDIDATE: I am.

Bishop:

Are you resolved to discharge the office of deacon with humility and love to assist the bishop and the priests and to serve all people?

CANDIDATE: I am.

Bishop:

Are you resolved to hold the mystery of the faith with a clear conscience, and to proclaim this faith in word and action?

CANDIDATE: I am.

Bishop:

Are you resolved to share God's unconditional love with all people, always remembering to be like Christ to others?

CANDIDATE: I am.

Bishop:

Are you resolved to help the sick, the marginalised, the poor and all those who come to you in need, holding in your heart always the love of Christ?

CANDIDATE: I am.

Bishop:

Will you always safeguard the children, protect the vulnerable and provide for those with special needs?

CANDIDATE: I will

Bishop:

Will you challenge injustice and corruption and be a beacon of light and hope in the community, always acting with integrity and probity?

CANDIDATE: I will

Bishop:

Are you resolved to maintain and deepen a spirit of prayer appropriate to your way of life and, in keeping with what is required of you?

CANDIDATE: I am, with the help of God.

Bishop:

Will you thus strive to use worthily the powers to be entrusted to you?

CANDIDATE: I will

Bishop:

May God who has begun the good work in you bring it to fulfilment

Candidate:

God, I believe in you: increase my faith.
I trust in you: strengthen my trust.
I love you: let me love you more.
I am sorry for my sins: deepen my sorrow.
Guide me by your wisdom,

Correct me with your justice,
Comfort me with mercy,
Protect me with your power.
Enlighten my understanding,
Strengthen my will,
Purify my heart.
Let me see myself as I really am:
A pilgrim in this world,
A person called to respect and love.
All those whose lives I touch,
My friends and my enemies.
Help me to conquer anger with gentleness,
Greed with generosity,
Apathy with fervour.
Help me to forget myself
And reach out towards others.
Put me on guard against my human weaknesses.
Let me cherish your love for me,
And come at last to your salvation.
I surrender myself to be guided by your will.
Your grace and your love
Are wealth enough for me.
May I be made worthy of your calling.
Amen.

Bishop:

Let us pray that the all-loving God will
pour out blessing on the one

to be received into the holy order of deacons.

THE LITANY

God eternal, To thee we sing,
Unto thee our love we bring;
Through the world thy praises ring;
We are thine, O Trinity.

Gentle One, we hail thee here,
Recognise thy presence dear
Feel and know that thou art near
Keeping thus thy promise

From our forebears we have heard
Of the gift thy hand conferred
We have proved thy holy word
Be that gift out poured

We this power would now convey
Strengthen thou our hands we pray
Pour thy grace through us today
Hear us Holy Comforter

Monarch, at thy feet we kneel
For this deacon we appeal
Fill her/his heart with holy zeal
In thy service Saviour

Thou of holy church the head
Mystic power upon her/him shed

By thy love may s/he be led
Hear us holy redeemer

Link in mystic bond with thee
This your deacon may s/he be
From the world and self set free
By thy power O Holy One

<u>The following verses as sung by the consecrating bishop alone</u>

We beseech thee hear our prayer
Bless + thy beloved prostrate there
Hold her/him in thy loving care
Hear us holy Trinity

Hear thy beloved as s/he prays
Help thy faithful one/s today
Love + and + life may s/he convey
Hear us holy Trinity

Pour thy loving kindness great
On this beloved candidate
Bless + her/him, + hallow, + consecrate.
Hear us holy Trinity.

<u>All say/ sing the last verse together</u>

God creator seen of none
God the co-eternal One
God the Spirit, one whole sum
We are thine O Trinity.

Bishop:

Prayer of Consecration

Loving God,
Be present with us.
You are the source of all that is.
You watch over all creation and make it new
Through Jesus Christ, your Word, your power,
And your wisdom.
You foresee all things in your eternal providence
And make due provision for every age.
You make the Church, Christ's body,
Grow to its full stature as a new
And greater temple
You enrich it with every kind of grace
And perfect it with a diversity of members
To serve the whole body
In a wonderful pattern of unity.
You established a threefold ministry of worship
And service for the glory of your name.
Look with favour on (-),
Whom we now dedicate to the office of deacon,
Send forth upon her/him
the Holy Spirit,
That s/he may be strengthened
By the gift of your grace
To carry out faithfully the work of the ministry.

May s/he excel in every virtue:
In love that is sincere,
In concern for the sick and the poor,
In unassuming authority,
In self-discipline,
And in holiness of life.
May her/his conduct
exemplify your commandments
And lead your people
to imitate her/his purity of life.
May s/he remain strong and steadfast in Christ,
Giving to the world the witness
of a pure conscience.
May s/he in this life imitate Jesus,
Who came, not to be served but to serve.

All: Amen.

In silence the bishop lays both hands on the head of CANDIDATE. The same is done after her/him successively by all the deacons/priests/bishops present and by others from the congregation.

Then when this is over, both the bishops and the clergy and the people, having their right hands extended towards the candidate, the bishop says the following:

Bishop:

God, whose strength is in the silence, grant that this your servant whom you join unto yourself in the holy bond of the diaconate may ever minister faithfully in your name. Amen.

Let us pray, that God may multiply the gifts of the Spirit in this disciple for the work of the diaconate.

THE VENI CREATOR

Come, thou Creator Spirit blest,
And in our souls take up thy rest.
Come with thy grace and
heavenly aid,
To fill the hearts which thou hast made.

Great Paraclete, to thee we cry,
O highest gift of God most high.
O living fount, O fire, O love
And sweet anointing from above.

Thou in thy sevenfold gift art known.
Thee, finger of God's hand, we own.
The promise of the Creator, thou
Who dost the tongue with power endow.

Kindle our senses from above
And make our hearts o'erflow with love.
With patience firm and virtue high
The weakness of our flesh supply.

Far let us drive our tempting foe
And thine abiding peace bestow.
So shall we not, with thee for guide,
Turn from the path of life aside.

O may thy grace on us bestow
The Creator and Love to know
And thee, through endless time confessed,
Of both eternal Spirit blest.

All glory while the ages run
Be to the Creator and the One,
Who gave us life; the same to thee,
O Holy Ghost, eternally. Amen.

Bishop: Receive the Holy Spirit for the office and work of a deacon in the church of God.

Bishop: O God the source of all holiness, source of true consecration and the fullness of spiritual benediction, we pray to + open to your heavenly grace, the heart and mind of (-), who has been raised to the diaconate, that through her/him your power may abundantly flow for the service of your people. May s/he be earnest and zealous as a fellow worker in our order and thus prove her/himself worthy of the sacred charge committed unto her/him. May s/he be ever watchful that s/he keeps the vessel of her/his ministry pure and undefiled. May every kind of righteousness spring forth within her/him and may her/his heart be so filled with compassion for the multitude that s/he may forget her/himself in love of others. May the radiance of your love and glory shine ever more brightly in her/his heart till, steadfast in your most joyous service, s/he shall rise unto spiritual maturity, unto the measure of the stature of the fullness of Christ, when her/his life shall be hid with Christ in God. Amen.

Bishop: Take this white + stole for a symbol of your office; remembering that as for the service and love of all people you do exercise the power which now is in you, so will it flow through you in ever greater fullness and glory. In the name of the + Creator and of the + Redeemer and of the + Holy Spirit.
Amen.

Bishop: The Lord clothe you with the vesture of gladness and ever encompass you with the dalmatic of justice, that you may work and

minister for a better more equal world in which all are welcomed, included, and enabled to fulfil their best. In the name of the + Creator and of the + Redeemer and of the + Holy Spirit.
Amen.

Bishop: Receive the Gospel of Christ, whose herald you now are. Believe what is true, teach what you believe, and practice what you teach. In the name of the + Creator and of the + Redeemer and of the + Holy Spirit. **Amen.**

THE COMMUNION CONTINUES

FOR PRIESTLY ORDINATIONS PRECEDED BY A BRIEF DIACONAL ORDINATION

The regular ordination service up to this point, then:

Presenter: We ask that you would now ordain this candidate here present to the order of the diaconate and the priesthood.

Bishop. Do you know her/him to be worthy?

As far as human frailty allows me to judge, I do both know and attest that s/he is worthy of the charge of this office.

Bishop. Thanks be to God.

Bishop: If anyone has any reason to believe that this ordination should not proceed, and that this person should not be ordained as a deacon and priest, then let them boldly come forward and present their reasons. However, let them first consider their own integrity and motivation.

Then will you, gathered here today, support her/him in her/his ministry?

Bishop: Dearly beloved, you who are about to be raised to the order of the diaconate, endeavour to receive this gift worthily and blamelessly. You must strive to rid yourselves of all unworthy propensities: Be seemly, courteous in demeanour, full of virtuous desires and manifesting a great love for God and all people. Demonstrate by your life and actions, the gospel, your lips will proclaim, that of you it may be said: "How beautiful upon the mountains is the one that brings good news; that comes to establish peace."

Bishop: Receive the Holy Spirit for the office and work of a deacon in the church of God.

Take this white stole as a symbol of your commission to be a channel of outpouring love for God and all people.

May you always be clothed with the vesture of hope and encompassed with the dalmatic of justice.

Take authority to declare the Gospel of Love and nourish hungry minds and lost souls with the living Word.

Then to the priestly charge.

FOR PRIESTLY ORDINATIONS

The regular ordination service up to this point, then:

Presenter: We ask that you would now ordain this candidate here present to the order of the priesthood.

Bishop. Do you know her/him to be worthy?

As far as human frailty allows me to judge, I do both know and attest that s/he is worthy of the charge of this office.

Bishop. Thanks be to God.

Bishop: If anyone has any reason to believe that this ordination should not proceed, and that this person should not be ordained as a priest, then let them boldly come forward and present their reasons. However, let them first consider their own integrity and motivation.

Then will you, gathered here today, support her/him in her/his ministry?

The Charge

Beloved (-), it is now my responsibility, to charge you with the gravity of the office and responsibility that you are about to receive as a priest.

Priests are called to devote their lives in service to God and all people. They will bless, forgive, confront, challenge, preside, preach, anoint, and make available, the unconditional love of God, to all, especially those who languish within this world.

They must commend themselves by their wisdom, integrity, compassion, honesty, and their concern for justice.

The fruits of their goodness must be evident in their lives: In their manner of speaking, their habits and choices, their relationships and social involvement.

They must strive, without ceasing, to increase within themselves the perfection of God's Love, that they may bear that Divine Love to all.

Never forget how great a privilege it is to help others. Priests must resist the evil that entraps and liberate those who have fallen captive to the world's darkness. They must lift the heavy burden of sorrow and sin from people's lives and avail them of the healing grace of forgiveness.

Priests must welcome all to be cleansed through the waters of baptism, and to receive the sacred mysteries, of the spiritual food and drink that Jesus's Love shares.

Priests must bring to the lost, beleaguered, and lonely, blessing and consolation, hope and strength, comfort, and renewed purpose, that the sweet savour of their lives will be a fragrance within this world.

Priests must strive always to reach out to the ostracised and dejected, easing the suffering of the weak, challenging and overcoming injustice and healing the broken hearted.

So, by their words and actions, they may be living expressions of God's Love.

The ordinand rises.

Before you are ordained a priest, you must declare before the people your intention to undertake this office. Are you willing to be ordained for the Church's ministry by the laying on of hands and the gift of the Holy Spirit?

CANDIDATE: I am.

Bishop:

Are you resolved to discharge the office of a priest with humility and love to assist the bishop and the priests and to serve all people?

CANDIDATE: I am.

Bishop:

Are you resolved to hold the mystery of the faith with a clear conscience, and to proclaim this faith in word and action?

CANDIDATE: I am.

Bishop:

Are you resolved to share God's unconditional love with all people, always remembering to be like Christ to others?

CANDIDATE: I am.

Bishop:

Are you resolved to help the sick, the marginalised, the poor and all those who come to you in need, holding in your heart always the love of Christ?

CANDIDATE: I am.

Bishop:

Will you always safeguard the children, protect the vulnerable and provide for those with special needs?

CANDIDATE: I will

Bishop:

Will you challenge injustice and corruption and be a beacon of light and hope in the community, always acting with integrity and probity?

Bishop:

Are you resolved to maintain and deepen a spirit of prayer appropriate to your way of life and, in keeping with what is required of you?

CANDIDATE: I am, with the help of God.

Bishop:

Will you thus strive to use worthily the powers to be entrusted to you?

CANDIDATE: I will

Bishop:

May God who has begun the good work in you bring it to fulfilment

Candidate:

God, I believe in you: increase my faith.
I trust in you: strengthen my trust.
I love you: let me love you more.
I am sorry for my sins: deepen my sorrow.
Guide me by your wisdom,
Correct me with your justice,
Comfort me with mercy,
Protect me with your power.
Enlighten my understanding,
Strengthen my will,
Purify my heart.
Let me see myself as I really am:
A pilgrim in this world,
A person called to respect and love.
All those lives I touch,
My friends and my enemies.
Help me to conquer anger with gentleness,
Greed with generosity,
Apathy with fervour.
Help me to forget myself
And reach out towards others.

Put me on guard against my human weaknesses.
Let me cherish your love for me,
And come at last to your salvation.
I surrender myself to be guided by your will.
Your grace and your love
Are wealth enough for me.
May I be made worthy of your calling.
Amen.

Bishop:

Let us pray that the all-loving God will
pour out blessing on (-), to be received into the
holy order of the priesthood.

THE LITANY

God eternal, to thee we sing,
Unto thee our love we bring.
Through the world thy praises ring.
We are thine, O Trinity.

Gentle One, we hail thee here,
Recognise thy presence dear
Feel and know that thou art near
Keeping thus thy promise

From our forebears we have heard
Of the gift thy hand conferred

We have proved thy holy word
Be that gift out poured

We this power would now convey
Strengthen thou our hands we pray
Pour thy grace through us today
Hear us Holy Comforter

Monarch, at thy feet we kneel
For this deacon we appeal
Fill her/his heart with holy zeal
In thy service Saviour

Thou of holy church the head
Mystic power upon her/him shed
By thy love may s/he be led
Hear us holy redeemer

Link in mystic bond with thee
This your deacon may s/he be
From the world and self set free
By thy power O Holy One

<u>The following verses as sung by the consecrating bishop alone</u>

We beseech thee hear our prayer
Bless + thy beloved prostrate there
Hold her/him in thy loving care
Hear us holy Trinity

Hear thy beloved as s/he prays

Help thy faithful one today
Love + and + life may s/he convey
Hear us holy Trinity

Pour thy loving kindness great
On this beloved candidate
Bless + her/him, + hallow, + consecrate;
Hear us holy Trinity.

<u>All say/ sing the last verse together</u>

God creator seen of none
God the co-eternal One
God the Spirit, one whole sum
We are thine O Trinity.

Prayer of Consecration

Loving God,
Be present with us.
You are the source of all that is.
You watch over all creation and make it new
Through Jesus Christ, your Word, your power,
and your wisdom.
You foresee all things in your eternal providence
And make due provision for every age.
You make the Church, Christ's body,
Grow to its full stature
As a new and greater temple.
You enrich it with every kind of grace

And perfect it with a diversity of members
To serve the whole body
In a wonderful pattern of unity.
You established a threefold
Ministry of worship and
Service for the glory of your name.
Look with favour on (-)
Whom we now dedicate to the office of a priest
Send forth upon her/him the Holy Spirit,
That s/he may be strengthened
By the gift of your grace
To carry out faithfully the work of the ministry.
May s/he excel in every virtue:
In love that is sincere,
In concern for the sick and the poor,
In unassuming authority,
In self-discipline,
And in holiness of life.
May her/his conduct exemplify your
Commandments
And lead your people to imitate her/his purity of life.
May s/he remain strong and steadfast in Christ,
Giving to the world the witness of a pure
Conscience.
May s/he in this life imitate Jesus,
Who came, not to be served but to serve.
All: Amen.

In silence the bishop lays both hands on the head of the deacon. The same is done after her/him successively by all the deacons/priests/bishops present, and others from the congregation.

When this is over, both the bishops and the clergy and the people, having their right hands extended towards the deacon, the bishop says the following:

Bishop:

O Lord Christ, whose strength is in the silence, grant that (-) whom you join unto yourself in the holy bond of the priesthood may ever minister faithfully. Amen.

Let us pray, that almighty God may multiply the gifts of the Spirit in this deacon for the work of the priesthood.

THE VENI CREATOR

> Come, thou Creator Spirit blest,
> And in our souls take up thy rest.
> Come with thy grace and
> heavenly aid,

To fill the hearts which thou hast made.

Great Paraclete, to thee we cry,
O highest gift of God most high.
O living fount, O fire, O love
And sweet anointing from above.

Thou in thy sevenfold gift art known.
Thee, finger of God's hand, we own.
The promise of the Creator, thou
Who dost the tongue with power endow.

Kindle our senses from above
And make our hearts o'erflow with love.
With patience firm and virtue high
The weakness of our flesh supply.

Far let us drive our tempting foe
And thine abiding peace bestow.
So shall we not, with thee for guide,
Turn from the path of life aside.

O may thy grace on us bestow
The Creator and Love to know
And thee, through endless time confessed,
Of both eternal Spirit blest.

All glory while the ages run
Be to the Creator and the One,
Who gave us life; the same to thee,
O Holy Ghost, eternally. Amen.

The bishop rises and imposes her/his hands

Bishop: Receive the Holy Spirit for the office and work of a priest in the church of God.

The bishop with hands extended towards the ordinand continues:

O God the source of all holiness, source of true consecration and the fullness of spiritual benediction, we pray to be + open to your heavenly grace the heart and mind of this your beloved, who has been raised to the priesthood, that through her/him your power may abundantly flow for the service of all people. May s/he be earnest and zealous as a fellow worker in our order and thus prove her/himself worthy of the sacred charge committed unto her/him. And, as s/he now shall provide for the service of your people, spiritual food, and drink, may s/he be ever watchful that s/he keeps the vessel of her/his ministry pure and undefiled.

May every kindness and righteousness spring forth within her/him and may her/his heart be so filled with compassion for the multitude that s/he may forget her/himself in the love of others. May the radiance of your love and glory shine ever more brightly in her/his heart till, steadfast in your service, s/he shall rise unto spiritual maturity, unto the measure of the stature of the fullness of Christ. Amen.

The bishop, taking the stole, places it on the priest saying:

Take this stole, for a symbol of the grace of the priestly office and as a channel of the everflowing stream of Christ's love.

The bishop vests the priest with the chasuble, saying:

Take the priestly vestment, the garment of Love, that wearing it, many will recognise and receive the sacred spiritual sustenance of Christ and be transformed.

The bishop anoints the hands of the new priest with the holy oil of catechumens, saying:

Be pleased, to consecrate and hallow these hands by this anointing and our + blessing; that whatsoever they + bless may be blessed and whatsoever they + consecrate may be consecrated and hallowed, in the name of Christ. Amen.

The bishop delivers a chalice containing wine and water, with a paten and host upon it saying:

Take authority to celebrate the Holy Eucharist for a hungry, thirsty, and needy world. Amen.

THE COMMUNION SERVICE CONTINUES

THE CONSECRATION OF A BISHOP

The regular ordination service up to this point, then:

Presenter: We ask that you would now consecrate this priest here present, to the charge of the Episcopate.

Bishop. Do you know her/him to be worthy?

As far as human frailty allows me to judge, I do both know and attest that s/he is worthy of the charge of this office.

Bishop. Thanks be to God.

Bishop: If anyone has any reason to believe that this consecration should not proceed, and that this person should not be consecrated as a bishop, then let them boldly come forward and present their reasons. However, let them first consider their own integrity and motivation.

Then will you, gathered here today, support her/him in her/his ministry?

Let the protocol of election be read.

It is required that those who are elected to the episcopal order shall be beforehand diligently examined to ensure they have the virtues suitable to this charge.

In God's name, therefore, we ask you, well beloved sister/brother whether, if you are consecrated to this sacred charge, you will exercise its powers wholly for what is good for others and will bring Love and benefit to them, and for no other purpose whatsoever, laying aside utterly all thought of personal advantage,

With my whole heart I will endeavour to do so.

Will you, so far as it is possible, focus your attention on what is good and virtuous and not on the temptations within the darkness.

I will

Will you, with God's help, remember that in this important office to which you are called, it is your duty and must be your constant care to show an example of godly life to all others.

I will

Will you ever respect as a sacred trust the power to be committed to you and solemnly pledge to exercise great care and discretion in the choice of those upon whom in Christ's name you shall bestow the gift of holy orders?

I will

Will you be always prepared to help and serve all people, so far as you are able, remembering that the most significant role of a bishop is to be exemplary in the practice of Love, compassion, and goodness.

I will

Will you seek always to be gentle and tender to the suffering, the sorrowful and those in need.

I will

Will you always safeguard children, respect, cherish and guide them?

I will

Will you protect the vulnerable and ensure provision is made for those with special needs?

I will

Will you be vigilant in identifying all that oppresses and courageous in resisting and overcoming abuse?

I will

Will you act with integrity, root out corruption, challenge the misuse of power and ensure that all you do, ministerially and personally, is above reproach.

I will

May God keep you true in all these things, well beloved sister/brother, and strengthen you in all goodness. Amen

THE COLLECT

Loving God, by whose spirit we are restored and blessed, impart your sanctifying grace to (-), who is to be numbered among the bishops of your church, that with a pure heart and open mind s/he may faithfully receive the gift of the Holy Spirit; through Christ, our Saviour.

THE FIRST READING

The Episcopal Charge

Bishops are called to be exemplars of Love, reflecting the life and grace of Jesus.

They should have attained a maturity of spirit and understanding whereby they can differentiate between what is true and false, discerning what lies behind the outward form.

They have eyes that see through the superficial and ears that hear beyond the noise of words, and all that competes for their attention.

They have a mind crafted by Love, to identify integrity and resist artifice.

They are not dependent on anything or anyone for their wellbeing but are sustained by God, Love, and virtue.

They are not susceptible to the transitory influences of fashion, opinion, or politics, but instead are rooted in knowledge based, rational and moral thinking.

They do not court popularity or crave fame or advancement. Their desire is to serve and minister, enhancing the lives of others and bringing blessing to the community.

They are to be shining lights, representing our best; kind, considerate, thoughtful, sensitive, measured, self-controlled, disciplined, compassionate, informed, and wise.

They are to resist corruption, challenge malpractice and work tirelessly for justice. Their commission is to help heal the sick, liberate the oppressed, enlighten the prejudiced and overcome conflict.

They should be symbols of unity and reconciliation, building bridges across divides, soothing enmities, leading the way to community harmony and peace, based on respect for all.

They are to treat every person with equal dignity, availing them of every spiritual and physical assistance necessary.

They are to have the care of souls of every person in the world, irrespective of their background, faith, or beliefs.

They are to Love with the unconditional, infinite, and extravagant measure that God loves us.

Then let us pray, that God in loving kindness and watchful care, may bestow upon (-) an abundance of grace for her/his future ministry.

> God eternal, to thee we sing,
> Unto thee our love we bring.
> Through the world thy praises ring.
> We are thine, O Trinity.

Gentle One, we hail thee here,
Recognise thy presence dear
Feel and know that thou art near
Keeping thus thy promise

From our forebears we have heard
Of the gift thy hand conferred
We have proved thy holy word
Be that gift out poured

We this power would now convey
Strengthen thou our hands we pray
Pour thy grace through us today
Hear us Holy Comforter

Monarch, at thy feet we kneel
For this priest we appeal
Fill her/his heart with holy zeal
In thy service Saviour

Thou of holy church the head
Mystic power upon her/him shed
By thy love may s/he be led
Hear us holy redeemer

Link in mystic bond with thee
This your priest may s/he be
From the world and self set free
By thy power O Holy One

<u>The following verses are sung by the consecrating bishop alone</u>

We beseech thee hear our prayer
Bless + thy beloved prostrate there
Hold her/him in thy loving care
Hear us holy Trinity

Hear thy beloved as s/he prays
Help thy faithful one today
Love + and + life may s/he convey
Hear us holy Trinity

Pour thy loving kindness great
On this beloved candidate
Bless + her/him, + hallow, + consecrate.
Hear us holy Trinity.

<u>All say/ sing the last verse together</u>

God creator seen of none
God the co-eternal One
God the Spirit, one whole sum
We are thine O Trinity.

An open book of the gospels is held over the neck and shoulders of the bishop elect.

O loving Christ, the fountain of all goodness, who by the operation of the Holy Spirit has appointed various orders within your church and for its enrichment and strengthening has empowered some to excel in wisdom, others in devotion and many to be skilled in action, pour down upon (-) the fullness of the Holy Spirit, that s/he may be equipped to lead, guide and inspire by the example of her/his life, and to speak God's living words for our world today. Amen

THE VENI CREATOR

>Come, thou Creator Spirit blest,
>And in our souls take up thy rest.
>Come with thy grace and
>heavenly aid,
>To fill the hearts which thou hast made.
>
>Great Paraclete, to thee we cry,
>O highest gift of God most high.
>O living fount, O fire, O love
>And sweet anointing from above.
>
>Thou in thy sevenfold gift art known.
>Thee, finger of God's hand, we own.
>The promise of the Creator, thou
>Who dost the tongue with power endow.
>
>Kindle our senses from above
>And make our hearts o'erflow with love.
>With patience firm and virtue high
>The weakness of our flesh supply.
>
>Far let us drive our tempting foe
>And thine abiding peace bestow.
>So shall we not, with thee for guide,

Turn from the path of life aside.

O may thy grace on us bestow
The Creator and Love to know
And thee, through endless time confessed,
Of both eternal Spirit blest.

All glory while the ages run
Be to the Creator and the One,
Who gave us life; the same to thee,
O Holy Ghost, eternally. Amen.

Bishop/s: Receive the Holy Spirit for the office and work of a bishop in the church of God

O God the creator, the redeemer and the sanctifier, as you have now bestowed upon (-) your awesome power and have consecrated her/him as your representative and teacher, open + her/his heart and mind to your grace, that s/he may handle wisely the power s/he has received and, always mindful of you, may never seek her/his own acclaim, but only the joy of being able to administer Love in all its fullness to a broken and dejected world. Amen

The head of the bishop is bound with a cloth and s/he is/are anointed with holy chrism, that is poured out upon her/him.

May your head be anointed and consecrated with Love's blessing, so that the power which you receive may always flow from you in ever greater abundance to the people to whom you are sent. Amen

You who are wisdom, strength, and beauty, make yourself known in and through (-). Let your wisdom dwell in her/his mind and enlighten her/his understanding, that s/he may be true in her/his judgements and wise in her/his counsel, able to discern that which is good with a deep spiritual and human knowledge. May s/he be strong and courageous, sustaining others in the face of darkness and despondency, a tower of strength to those that are faltering. Let the beauty of holiness shine from her/him in her/his conversation and actions. May s/he be reverent, devout, and steadfast in the service of all people. May gentleness adorn her/his life so that s/he may win the hearts of others and open them to the light. Above all, may s/he be so filled with Love, that s/he may so touch hearts that many will be rescued from the darkness and be brought into Love's marvellous light. Amen

The hands of the bishop are anointed

May these hands be consecrated and hallowed for your work and ministry as a bishop, by this anointing, with the holy chrism of salvation. In the name of the Creator+, the Redeemer+, and the Sanctifier+. Amen

The sign of the cross is made over the heart and then of the hands of the bishop

May you overflow with spiritual blessing, so that what you bless + may be blessed and what you hallow may be hallowed and that the laying on of these consecrated hands will impart life and power to the people. Amen

The bishop holding the new bishop's pastoral staff prays:

May this staff be a symbol of guidance, direction, support, and power and be handled with humility and grace. Amen

And holding the cross, prays:

May this potent symbol of Love's willingness to endure suffering, in the pursuit of goodness and justice, ever be an inspiration to the one who wears it, as to all those who behold it. Amen.

And holding the ring, prays:

May this ring ever wed the bearer to Love's endeavour and ever commit her/his hands to fashion the earth anew to God's design and ever direct her/his heart to regard all creation as precious, encircled in golden light. Amen

The staff is presented to the new bishop:

Receive this staff and walk with it only on the paths of goodness, that encountering the pitfalls of injustice, it will steady you, and coming to many crossroads, it will guide you, and being confronted by evil, it will empower you.

The cross is presented to the new bishop:

Receive this cross, that wearing it, you will bear the weight of past suffering, declare your own commitment to resist wickedness, irrespective of the cost and display through your life, the living proof, that Love has the grace to vanquish all the instruments of death.

The ring is presented to the new bishop:

Receive this ring, that wearing it, you assure everyone, without exception or partiality, that you are committed to their highest and best, and have been sent to their hearts to bring them healing, blessing and life.

The Book of the Gospel is presented to the new bishop:

As these words have been hitherto delivered to bring life and joy, let your words be a source of divine instruction, guidance, and life.

The consecrating bishop says:

Peace be with you

And also with you

THE SERVICE OF HOLY COMMUNION CONTINUES

After the final blessing of the service:

The consecrating bishop blesses the mitre and gloves of the new bishop and then places the mitre on the new bishop:

Receive this mitre. May it channel the grace and power of Love through you to many, a symbol of the anointing inspiration bestowed upon all who offer themselves in Love's service. May its height elevate people's eyes to the highest and to their highest and its splendour motivate all to attain their best, with the promise that therein alone awaits our ultimate fulfilment.

The new bishop covers his hands with the gloves:

Wear these gloves, as a sign that you must always strive to maintain a purity of spirit, motivation and intention and never sully the loving path upon which you have been called. You are to be a beacon of light, shining brightly.

The new bishop/s is/are seated in the sanctuary:

O loving God, strengthen and resource (-) that s/he may govern those entrusted to her/his care with humility, gentleness, and grace, not lauding it over others, but rather laying down her/his life in compassionate and committed service. In the name of Jesus, Amen

The new bishop gives the final blessing.

THE 39 ARTICLES OF MODERN CHRISTIANITY

I. OF FAITH IN THE HOLY TRINITY

There is one God of infinite power, wisdom and goodness, the creator and preserver of all things, visible and invisible. And this one God encompasses a complex community in whom all are united.

II. OF THE WORD OR 'SON OF GOD' AND 'DAUGHTER OF GOD'.

Jesus is referred to as 'the son' of God and the 'word' of God. While being fully human, he was recognised as representing God and God's words, in such a way, that those who experienced him, felt they were in God's presence. He was identified as an exemplar that human nature and divine nature can be united in us. Mary, his mother, can be referred to as the 'daughter of God' whose life and love were so pure and so divine that she raised Jesus to perfection and God's 'word' was found in her and delivered through her.

III. OF THE GOING DOWN OF CHRIST INTO HELL

Jesus was described as 'the anointed one', the Christ'. He challenged secular and religious corruption and the misuse of power. For this he was arrested and crucified. He died and was buried. This path of suffering meant that he experienced hell on earth.

IV. OF THE RESURRECTION OF CHRIST

Death could not contain the Love that Jesus had demonstrated in his life and this Love rose anew from the grave, in such a way, that his life was resurrected in the lives of his followers.

V. OF THE HOLY SPIRIT

The Holy Spirit describes the divine inspiration that sanctifies us and empowers us to live good and loving lives.

VI. OF THE RESOURCE OF THE HOLY SCRIPTURES IN OUR RECEIPT OF SALVATION

Parts of Holy Scripture and much inspirational writing contain vital resources to assist us in learning and our following those things necessary to salvation.

VII. OF THE 'OLD TESTAMENT'

The 'Old Testament' charts the development of religious and spiritual understanding through history, as people strove to make sense of their lives and opportunities. All scripture must be read with a discerning and informed understanding to glean the acquired wisdom that emerges. The ten commandments provide an essential foundation for morality.

VIII. OF THE THREE CREEDS

The three ancient creeds, The Nicene, Athanasian and Apostle's creed are the historic deposit of the Christian tradition, that reflect the understanding of the time that they were written.

IX. OF SIN

We have the potential for good or evil. When we can choose, we become responsible for our choices. Choosing what is right can involve conflict with what we would prefer to do. We must learn to discipline ourselves to resist the temptation towards evil.

X. OF FREE-WILL

We have free will. There are many things and people, that can influence us towards good or evil, and as we mature, we can identify those resources that will strengthen our resolve to choose goodness, not least among them our Christian faith.

XI. OF THE JUSTIFICATION OF WOMEN AND MEN

Jesus has exemplified the way of righteousness. In following him, we are instructed in holiness. We experience disappointment and failure but also the resolve to keep persevering. In this endeavour we are justified before God not because of our sincere achievements, though they are important, but because of our faith in God's mercy.

XII. OF GOOD WORKS

Our good works, which are the fruits of faith, and follow Justification, are the evidence of our sincerity, as the fruit from a tree indicates its wellbeing.

XIII. OF WORKS BEFORE JUSTIFICATION

Any good work is pleasing to God and a sign of the inspiration of God's spirit.

XIV. OF WORKS OF SUPEREROGATION

We are encouraged to work tirelessly for good throughout our lives, not becoming arrogant or boastful about our kindnesses, but in humility and out of love, doing all we can to help transform the world for the better.

XV. OF CHRIST AND SIN

Jesus, being fully human, shared the same struggles known to us, and sinned as we do. If any person claims they have no sin, they are mistaken, and the truth is not in them. Jesus matured well to be able to contain the propensity to sin and to live in the light. He taught us how to grow to a position where we can help in removing sin from the world.

XVI. OF SIN AFTER BAPTISM

When we sin, we must repent and receive forgiveness and commit ourselves anew to the path of goodness.

XVII. OF PREDESTINATION AND ELECTION

It is God's predestined purpose that all should be saved. We are elected to be God's children, called to learn how to resist unworthy desires and aspire always towards high and holy aims. We must be comforted that God promises us grace and the enabling power of the Holy Spirit to aid our endeavours.

XVIII. OF OBTAINING ETERNAL SALVATION BY THE NAME OF CHRIST

There are many ways to discover and walk faithfully on the paths of goodness. Hearkening to the message of Jesus and following his teaching is one such and will lead us to that holy place wherein we will find hope, strength, and abundant life.

XIX. OF THE CHURCH

The visible church of Christ is found in the hearts of all those faithful women and men who walk the Christian way in holiness of life. Their deeds are one with the word of God preached; and their outreach, providing sustenance to the poor and needy, one with the sacraments received.

XX. OF THE AUTHORITY OF THE CHURCH

The community of Christians, called the church, has the power to guide and direct the growth of Christianity. However, its evolution must always be in accordance with the mandate of Love.

XXI. OF THE AUTHORITY OF GENERAL COUNCILS

Large ecumenical gatherings of Christians can determine matters pertaining to the church, however only in accordance with Love, justice, and truth.

XXII. OF PURGATORY AND HELL

Christians should not speculate about matters beyond our knowledge and experience and should refrain from constructing beliefs based around imagination. Hell, and purgatory describe states that our choices deliver us into, through our human experience, because of the consequences of our wrongdoing. In contrast, it is our lifetime commission to do our utmost to create heaven upon the earth.

XXIII. OF MINISTERING IN THE CONGREGATION

Any women or man, who is regarded with respect and recognised as one striving to follow the Christian way, can be invited to assist in worship. Certain among them may be called by God and authorised by the community to lead a congregation.

XXIV. OF SPEAKING IN THE CONGREGATION IN SUCH A TONGUE AS THE PEOPLE UNDERSTAND

The language and rituals used in worship and in public gatherings should generally be understandable to those involved.

XXV. OF THE SACRAMENTS

Sacraments are effective signs of grace and God's good will towards us, by which we are invisibly strengthened and renewed in our faith, hope and resolve. There are many sacraments, among them Baptism and Jesus's Supper.

XXVI. OF THE UNWORTHINESS OF THE MINISTERS, WHICH HINDERS NOT THE EFFECT OF THE SACRAMENT

At times evil can infiltrate a person and a community, however such evil can never eradicate the essence of goodness that is contained in all that which is good, nor can it remove the efficacy of that goodness from any sacrament that has been delivered unto others. However, such evil must be exposed and dealt with rapidly and effectively.

XXVII. OF BAPTISM

Baptism is a sign of new birth and regeneration. The baptised person is welcomed into the visible church as a daughter or son of God and receives the forgiveness of her/his sins and the comfort of the Holy Spirit.

XXVIII. OF JESUS'S SUPPER

Jesus's supper is a sign of the love that Christians ought to have among themselves for one another and the love they ought to have for all people. It is also how Christians share in the continuing life of Jesus.

XXIX. OF EVIL THAT PARTAKES OF JESUS'S SUPPER.

No benefit, of itself is gained by partaking of the sacrament without faith and holiness.

XXX. OF BOTH KINDS

Both the food and the drink of the sacrament should be offered to all people, of any age, including and especially, all the children. (The wine can be replaced with a suitable alternative, like blackcurrant juice.).

XXXI. OF THE OBLATION OF CHRIST UPON THE CROSS

Jesus demonstrated unconditional and sacrificial love in response to the sins he encountered in the world. His example provided an eternal model for us to emulate in our exposure to sin

XXXII. OF THE MARRIAGE OF PRIESTS

Clergy are free to marry a partner, of the same or opposite gender, should they choose.

XXXIII. OF EXCOMMUNICATION

The church has no authority to excommunicate

XXXIV. OF THE TRADITIONS OF THE CHURCH

Uniformity is not required in worship, prayer, and ritual.

XXXV. OF THE HOMILIES

There are countless erudite and inspirational books and writing to aid the Christian in enhancing and developing their Christian life.

XXXVI. OF CONSECRATION OF BISHOPS AND MINISTERS

The Consecration of archbishops and bishops and the ordaining of priests and deacons must be done with due process, and careful attention to ensure the integrity of all so raised.

XXXVII. OF THE AUTHORITIES

Christians should always be law abiding and model citizens as long, as the authorities are acting according to law, in pursuit of the common good and upholding the principles of justice and truth.

XXXVIII. OF CHRISTIAN PEOPLE'S GOODS

Every Christian ought to be generous in giving to charities and the poor, according to their means.

XXXIX. OF A CHRISTIAN PERSON'S OATH

A Christian can swear an oath in a court of law, though generally their words should always be true, thus negating the need to speak other than plainly.

THE AUTHOR'S BIOGRAPHY

Archbishop Jonathan Blake has lived a fascinating life, dedicated to helping others. You can read about him on his web site: www.bishopjonathanblake.com

You are welcome to email him at:

archbishopjonathanblake@gmail.com

Printed in Great Britain
by Amazon